# Starring Quincy
# Rumpel

**Collect all the Quincy Rumpel books!**

*Quincy Rumpel*
*Starring Quincy Rumpel*
*Quincy Rumpel, P.I.*
*Morris Rumpel and the Wings of Icarus*
*Quincy Rumpel and the Sasquatch of Phantom Cove*
*Quincy Rumpel and the Woolly Chaps*

# Starring Quincy Rumpel

## by Betty Waterton

A Groundwood Book
Douglas & McIntyre
TORONTO/VANCOUVER/BUFFALO

Groundwood Books/Douglas & McIntyre
585 Bloor Street West
Toronto, Ontario M6G 1K5

The publisher gratefully acknowledges the assistance of
the Ontario Arts Council and the Canada Council.

Canadian Cataloguing in Publication Data

Waterton, Betty
    Starring Quincy Rumpel

ISBN 0-88899-196-7

I. Title.

PS8595.A84S8 1993    jC813'.54    C93-094903-X
PZ7.W38St 1993

Design by Michael Solomon
Cover art by Eric Beddows
Printed and bound in Canada

To my family, with love.

# 1

# Some Lost Cords

"HAS ANYBODY SEEN MY NEW CORDS?"

Quincy's voice rang out loud and clear from the upstairs landing, but no one was listening.

Outside, as the September sun filtered through patches of early morning fog, most of Tulip Street was just beginning to stir. But in the Rumpels' rambling old brown house at Number 57, things were already hopping.

In the kitchen a radio blared the weather report while Mrs. Rumpel prepared breakfast amid a clatter of pots and pans. She was being assisted by Morris, the youngest Rumpel. Morris had recently taken an interest in cooking and was now trying to smooth out the lumps in a pot of oatmeal.

Upstairs, in what he liked to think of as the master bedroom, Mr. Rumpel was roaming around humming happily to himself as he shaved with his electric razor. From the bathroom at the end of the hall came the sound of water running in the shower, and someone singing off-key. It was Leah, the middle Rumpel child.

Hanging over the bannister, clad in new white socks with maroon stripes, a Save-the-Whales T-shirt and her underwear, Quincy Rumpel was almost ready for school. Her cropped red hair had been neatly stuck down with Vaseline. Her rosy-hued, stainless-steel-rimmed glasses gleamed from a recent cleaning.

She had been up since six getting ready for her first day in grade seven. While the other Rumpels slumbered, she had showered, shampooed with a three-egg-and-olive-oil shampoo (her own recipe) and showered again. Until now, everything had been going nicely.

Receiving no reply to her cry of distress, Quincy pounded on the bathroom door, shouting, "Are my new cords in there?"

The singing stopped. "What?" a voice croaked.

Opening the door, Quincy poked her head in and was immediately engulfed in clouds of steam that came pouring over the top of the shower curtain.

"HAVE YOU SEEN MY MAROON CORDS?"

"YOUR BALLOON AWARDS?"

"Oh, never mind!"

Just then a mellow *bong, bong, bong*! rang through the house. It was the Rumpels' genuine Swiss cowbell. The family had brought it with them to the West Coast when they had moved from the east. Now it was proudly installed outside the front door of Number 57.

"Our cowbell's ringing!" cried Quincy, making a grab for the nearest towel. Twisting it about her waist, she sprinted for the stairs.

"I'll get it!" shrilled Morris, running from the kitchen with a wooden spoon in his hand.

"My rebounders!" exclaimed Mr. Rumpel. "It must be my rebounders!" Half-shaved, he bolted out of the bedroom and rushed down the stairs behind Quincy. At the bottom, they both collided with Morris.

"Did I hear the cowbell?" asked Mrs. Rumpel, sticking her head out of the kitchen. She stepped past the tangle of bodies at the bottom of the stairs and opened the front door. The verandah was heaped with cardboard boxes. They were large, square and flat.

"Good grief!" said Mrs. Rumpel.

"They're here!" cried Mr. Rumpel delightedly. "The Rumpel Rebounders are here!"

"Hurray!" shouted Quincy. "We're in business at last!"

"Are we ever! And when these 144 are sold, I'll order another 144!" Mr. Rumpel was gasping slightly as he staggered into the house under a load of the cartons.

"I hope you're not going to leave them in the living room," said Mrs. Rumpel as her husband began stacking them against one wall.

"They won't be here long," her husband assured her. "They'll sell like hotcakes—you wait and see!"

"I'll bet you'd sell a jillion if you advertised on TV," said Quincy, lugging two rebounders into the house. "If you like, I could help you advertise them. You wouldn't even have to pay me."

"Hee, hee!" snickered Morris. "You'd sure look funny on TV like that! Your towel's slipping, you know."

Hastily dropping the rebounders, Quincy clutched the towel around her middle. Glaring at Morris, she swept past him and up the stairs.

The rebounders were Mr. Rumpel's newest project. An earlier endeavour—mushroom farming in the garage—had been discontinued after suffering severe crop failure. The house at 57 Tulip Street had been selected mostly because its windowless garage had seemed ideal for growing mushrooms. Of course, it had many added bonuses, like a splendid cherry tree in the backyard and a plate rail in the dining room for Mr. Rumpel's doorknob collection. It was also near the beach, and not far from the Other Rumpels—Uncle George, Aunt Ida and Gwen.

10

"Open 'em up! Open 'em up!" Morris, who had disappeared briefly into the kitchen, was back jumping around and eating a peanut-buttered bagel as Mr. Rumpel began removing staples from a carton.

"Here it comes, everybody!" announced Mr. Rumpel, pulling out the contents with a flourish.

"*Ta-da*!" he cried, holding up a smallish, round, black mini-trampoline.

"That's it?" gasped Mrs. Rumpel, looking surprised.

"A genuine Rumpel Rebounder," said her husband proudly, "upon which the Rumpel fortunes may be founded!"

"The ones we had at school were huge," said Morris, hopping on. "Our whole class could get on at the same time."

"Ha! No way!" cried Quincy, who had reappeared wearing a pair of old gym shorts. "Anyway, nobody wants a giant trampoline in their living room."

"By the way," said Mr. Rumpel, "be careful where you use the rebounder in here. You don't want to jump up and hit your head on the chandelier." Many years before, when the brown house was being built, someone had made a mistake and installed a fancy crystal chandelier in the middle of the living-room ceiling. They had also made a mistake in the dining room. *It* had only a single, dangling light bulb.

Giving Morris a shove, Quincy hopped onto the rebounder. "I've done this lots of times," she told her parents. "Just watch me!" And she began a series of energetic leaps.

"Boing! Boing! Boing!" she hollered.

"Hey, our rebounders came!" cried Leah, running downstairs. Nine years old and dressed for school, she was wearing lace-trimmed ankle socks, a plaid skirt—handed down from her cousin Gwen (as good as new, said Mrs. Rumpel)—and a brand-new flowered blouse. Her fair hair had been brushed into two ponytails, firmly gripped in elastic bands decorated with blue plastic balls.

"Quincy! You're going to make us late!" she said when she saw her sister. Balanced precariously on one leg, Quincy was waving the other one in the air. Beneath her the rebounder quivered alarmingly.

"What are you doing?" asked Leah.

"A can-can kick," muttered Quincy, beginning to wobble.

"You're not even dressed!"

"I can't find my maroon cords."

"Have you lost them already?" cried Mrs. Rumpel. "They must be around somewhere. You haven't even worn them yet! Well, you'd better wear something else today. Those cords would be too warm, anyway. Now go and get your breakfast, all of you!'' And she made waving motions toward the kitchen.

Springing nimbly off the rebounder, Quincy felt her knees suddenly buckle under her. Picking herself up off the floor, she wailed, ''But I've got to have my maroon cords. I've been saving them new for school, and they match my socks!'' Still wearing her gym shorts, she trailed after the others.

With her family all in the kitchen or upstairs (Mr. Rumpel having returned to his shaving), Mrs. Rumpel stood alone in the living room, surveying it. Suddenly she hitched up the hem of her dressing gown in one hand and stepped gingerly onto the rebounder.

She took one careful little hop. Growing braver, she took several. Then, kicking off her slippers, she began to bounce up and down.

Flushed with excitement, she leaped with greater and greater abandon, her pink nightgown and terrycloth bathrobe swirling about her legs.

''Whoopeee!'' cried Mrs. Rumpel.

Slowly she became aware of voices coming from the kitchen. ''Hey, Mom! Morris ate all the bagels and the porridge is lumpy!''

''Lumpy, lumpy, lumpy!'' screeched Morris. ''You always say my porridge is lumpy!''

"MOTHER! There's no more bread!"

"Down in the freezer!" shouted Mrs. Rumpel, brushing the hair out of her eyes. But there was so much going on in the kitchen that no one heard her.

Sighing, she stepped carefully off the rebounder and retrieved her slippers. Then she went downstairs to the basement.

Lifting the lid of the freezer, she groped around inside for a loaf of bread. Instead, her fingers closed around something flat, hard and frosty. She pulled it out.

It seemed to be a slab of corduroy, covered with frost and hard as a rock.

Holding it out stiffly in front of her, Mrs. Rumpel marched upstairs and into the kitchen.

"My cords!" cried Quincy. "You found my cords!"

"Just tell me what they were doing in the freezer," begged her mother.

"Oh, gosh. I forgot I put them in there." Grabbing her pants, Quincy stretched them out on the counter and began picking at something in the pocket.

"I got my bubblegum stuck in here the other day when I was trying them on. I read somewhere that if you put gummy stuff in the freezer they're easy to unstick ... "

"Just hurry up, Quincy!" pleaded Leah. "We're going to be late!"

"Lunches!" cried Mrs. Rumpel suddenly. "We forgot to make lunches!"

"It's only a half-day today, Mother," Leah reminded her.

"Oh, that's right. Well, be sure and show Morris where the bathroom is at school. And don't forget to bring him home."

"Irony!" moaned Quincy, peeling gum out of the pocket of her cords. "Do you want to know what irony is, everybody? It's me being in the same school as Morris."

"What about me?" complained Leah. "I'm going to be stuck with him for the next three years!"

"Ma, they're talking about me again." Morris was rummaging in the bread box. "Are there any muffins?"

"You finished them last night. Have some more oatmeal."

"It's sorta lumpy."

Suddenly Quincy darted out of the kitchen. She reappeared just as suddenly, holding a hair dryer. Plugging it into an outlet, she began blow-drying her corduroy pants.

"Hurry up!" urged Leah. "We haven't got all day!"

"I'm coming! I'm coming! It's not working, anyway. I think it's broken. It only blows cold air."

Laying the hair dryer down in disgust, Quincy grabbed her cords and careened out of the kitchen, crashing into Mr. Rumpel on the way.

"What's the matter with her?" he asked, staggering against the door. He was clutching his calculator, hopefully estimating how many more rebounders he might need to order.

While Leah waited impatiently in the front hall for the others, Morris came drifting down the stairs.

"Did you go?" asked his mother.

"I couldn't. Quincy's still flushing her teeth."

"I know we're going to be late," fumed Leah. "I just know it! On the first day and everything!"

At last they heard the steps squeak, and down came Quincy. She had on a woollen orange ski sweater, her new socks, old jogging shoes and her maroon cords.

"You're walking funny," said Morris.

"You would be, too, if you had these pants on," replied Quincy. "They feel clammy."

"I still think you'll be too warm," said Mrs. Rumpel. "Weather Wilma said it's going to be a hot one today."

"I don't care," said Quincy, shuffling out the door after the others.

But as they hurried down Tulip Street, she began to moan and puff. "Phew!" she said. "It's warmer than I thought!"

"Mom said you'd be too hot," remarked Morris smugly.

"Get lost, Morris."

Gwen was waiting out in front of her house. She had on a flowered cotton skirt, sleeveless white blouse and sandals. Not even any socks, noted Quincy enviously.

"What's been keeping you?" asked Gwen. "I thought you were never coming!"

"Quincy lost her cords ... " began Leah.

"And our Rumpel Rebounders came. Hundreds and hundreds of 'em!" said Morris.

"Mom found them in the freezer, but then Quincy had to thaw them out ... " Leah continued.

"Morris's porridge was lumpy and he ate all the bagels, and the hair dryer only blew cold air and wouldn't thaw my pants," Quincy explained.

"Oh," said Gwen, looking vague.

By the time they reached the school, Quincy's face was pink and she was sweating. "Aren't you hot in those clothes?" asked Gwen.

"Not really," said Quincy grimly.

"You look hot," said Leah. "Why don't you take off your ski sweater? Just wear your Save-the-Whales T-shirt."

"I'm not hot!" said Quincy. "Anyway, I took my T-shirt off to save it."

"Haven't you got anything on under your ski sweater?" Gwen looked shocked.

"No. Nothing. Zilch."

"Ho, boy. You're going to be sorry!"

The school was new for Quincy, Leah and Morris, who had only moved to Tulip Street that summer. Gwen, however, quickly found Morris's grade two classroom and he was deposited in it, after the nearest bathroom was pointed out to him.

As they left him standing beside the teacher waiting to be assigned to a desk, Quincy turned to look back. Despite his new long pants and T-shirt with ATHLETIC DEPARTMENT printed on the back, Morris looked small and worried, she thought.

"Wait here afterwards," she called back to him. "I'll come and get you." Morris looked relieved.

"He's really pretty small," Quincy said to the others.

Next they left Leah with the grade fours, and by the time Quincy and Gwen found out they would be in the same class, Morris had been forgotten.

"Oh, good! We've got Miss Dingwall!" said Gwen.

"Ha-ha!" laughed Quincy. "Dingbat Dingwall! I can hardly wait. It's going to be so great being top dog this year!"

Miss Dingwall seated her pupils alphabetically, putting Quincy directly behind Gwen. "If you're a model student like your cousin," she told Quincy, "you'll be a real asset to the school." Gwen smiled modestly. Quincy beamed.

As the morning warmed up, Gwen noticed a peculiar smell coming from behind her. She turned to look, and there was Quincy fanning herself with her notebook. Her hair was stuck to her forehead in little strings. It smelled eggy.

"I'm dying," gasped Quincy, flapping the neck of her orange turtleneck ski sweater.

Miss Dingwall turned around from writing on the blackboard just as Quincy suddenly slumped back in her seat, her arms hanging limply at her sides. Her eyes were closed and her mouth was open.

"Quincy! Quincy Rumpel!" cried the teacher. "Are you all right?"

Quincy opened her eyes and looked around. Every single person in the room was staring at her.

"I'm just so hot, Miss Dingbat. You can't guess how hot I am."

Everybody snickered. "Quiet, please!" ordered Miss Dingwall. Then, turning to Quincy, she asked, "Why don't you take off that heavy sweater?"

"I can't," mumbled Quincy. "I just can't."

And so Quincy managed to make an impression on her new classmates, but not the kind she'd had in mind. After all, who wants to be remembered as the only kid in school wearing a ski sweater and clammy cords on what turned out to be the hottest September day in years?

# 2
# Puppies, Need Love

By the end of the week, things were settling down in the Rumpel house. Mr. Rumpel was busy selling his rebounders. Mrs. Rumpel was working (on rainy days) in Uncle George's umbrella shop. And Quincy, Leah and Morris were getting used to their new school.

"I think we can start looking for a dog now," Quincy said to Leah and Morris one morning at breakfast. "Mom and Dad said we might get a dog after things settled down, and they can't get much more settled than this."

As soon as the paper arrived that afternoon, Quincy leafed through it until she found the pet column. Sprawling out on the floor, she began to read. Suddenly she sprang up shouting, "Puppies! Here's some puppies in the paper, and *they need love!*"

"That sounds perfect!" cried Leah, kneeling down to look at the paper. Together they read the ad aloud. "Puppies, size medium, twenty dollars. Need love. 105 Otter Street."

"I hope that's not too far away," worried Leah.

"Nah. I think it's pretty close. And, boy, we can sure give 'em love!" Ripping the page out of the paper, Quincy and Leah raced to the kitchen to find their father. Because it was a rainy day and Mrs. Rumpel was working, Mr. Rumpel and Morris were making supper.

"Dad! We found our puppy!" cried Quincy, flapping the page at her father.

"I didn't know we'd lost one." Mr. Rumpel was sizzling some sausages in a pan while Morris sat on a chair with a bowl of pancake batter on his knees, slowly stirring it with a wooden spoon.

"Don't take all the lumps out," Leah told him. "Gwen says it should be lumpy."

"Lumpy, shlumpy. First you say my porridge is lumpy and now you say my pancakes aren't," grumbled Morris. "What did you say about a puppy?" Letting his spoon sink under the batter, he set the bowl down on the table and snatched the paper from Quincy.

"How about setting the table, girls?" asked Mr. Rumpel. "Meanwhile I'll show you how to make perfect pancakes. Just watch." Holding the bowl over the skillet, he was deftly pouring out the batter into even rounds when out slithered Morris's spoon.

By the time Mr. Rumpel had retrieved it, the pancakes had formed into a sticky, shapeless mass.

"Maybe you could cut them into squares," suggested Leah as Quincy grabbed the newspaper back from Morris. Tucking it under her arm, she proceeded to drop some knives and forks onto the table.

"Dad," pleaded Quincy, "they're size medium and they're only twenty dollars. Can I flip the pancakes?"

"Don't let her flip 'em, Dad," protested Morris. "She always messes them up."

Mr. Rumpel didn't answer. He was staring glumly at their rapidly congealing dinner.

Just then they heard the cowbell ringing frantically. "Mom's forgotten her keys again," said Quincy, sprinting to the front door. She was followed closely by Leah and Morris.

As Leah opened the door, Quincy waved the newspaper under her mother's nose. "Can we get one, Mom? Puppies, and they need love!"

"And they're only twenty dollars!" added Morris.

Mrs. Rumpel stood reading the ad while the rainwater dripped off her yellow plastic raincoat into a puddle on the floor. "I guess it wouldn't hurt to look," she said. "But I'm not promising. What does your father say?"

"Well, he didn't say no," Quincy told her.

As they ate their dinner that night, the three young Rumpels could think of nothing but dogs.

"I can't believe we're getting one at last," said Quincy.

"It's about time," mumbled Morris. "I'm almost into my puberty."

"Don't talk with your mouth full," said his mother. "These pancakes are quite different. I've never had square ones before."

"It might be kind of nice to have a dog," said Mr. Rumpel. "We always had one when I was growing up."

"Mom, there's no more syrup." Leah held the empty bottle upside down. "Look at Morris's plate. It's swimming!"

"I practically made supper," declared Morris. "Can't I have a little syrup?"

"All right, all right! There's more in the cupboard!"

As Mrs. Rumpel got up to get it, Quincy cried out, "Can we please hurry before they're all gone?"

"I hope they're beagles. Then we can call ours Snoopy," said Leah.

"How ordinaire!" scoffed Quincy.

"I'd call him Tramp." Morris scooped up the last of his syrup with a spoon.

Rolling her eyes upwards, Quincy implored the ceiling, "Mon stars! Give me strength!"

At last the Rumpels were finished supper. At exactly five minutes after six they piled into their ancient station wagon and set out, to get immediately caught up in the dinnertime traffic. When they were stopped at the fifth red traffic light, Quincy thought she would burst.

"You can go, Dad, you can go!" she urged. "It's only just turning red."

"I don't intend to get a traffic ticket over a dog we don't even have."

"But, Dad, they'll all be gone!" wailed the back-seat chorus.

But they weren't. Even though Otter Street turned out to be on the other side of town, when the Rumpels finally pulled into the driveway of 105 and hurried into the house, they found nine assorted puppies left—some black, some white and one white with black spots.

"They're a bit larger than I thought," said Mrs. Rumpel. "But they are awfully cute."

"Oh, one has spots!" cried Quincy. "I've always wanted one with spots!"

Leah thought she would like a white one, while Morris preferred black, to match the walls of his room. Mrs. Rumpel loved them all. As the puppies swarmed into their arms, Mr. Rumpel, in a weak moment, wondered about taking one of each.

"Only one!" Mrs. Rumpel said firmly. "But how are we ever going to choose?"

"I've read all about it," said Quincy. "You just pick the liveliest one with good conformation and a soft mouth."

"I think you're getting it mixed up with choosing a horse," said her father.

"What's conformation?" asked Morris.

"Shape," answered Quincy. "Something you won't have if you keep eating like that." Morris, who had brought along a leftover pancake to nibble on, was sending the puppies into a frenzy of excitement.

"Hurry up and finish it!" ordered Mr. Rumpel. Morris crammed the rest of the pancake into his mouth.

"Oh, gross!" groaned Leah.

As all the puppies had soft mouths and were the same shape—round—the Rumpels decided that they would go for the liveliest.

That turned out to be the spotted one, and he was soon on his way to Tulip Street in the back seat of the Rumpels' wagon. Quincy, in the middle, held most of the puppy on her lap, with Leah on one side stroking its head and Morris on the other, patting its tail.

"He's got seven spots," announced Quincy. "Counting the ones on his tummy. I wonder if he's a Dalmatian! Maybe he can go on TV with us when we advertise the rebounders. Wouldn't he be cute?''

"We could teach him tricks," said Leah.

"Oh, we would. We'll train him and everything."

"Just so long as you house-break him," warned their mother.

"Oh, we will!"

"I'll bet Mr. and Mrs. Murphy will be surprised when they hear we've got a dog!" said Morris.

As soon as they got home, he rushed next door to tell their neighbours. In a few minutes he was back.

"Mr. and Mrs. Murphy will be right over. They got real excited when I told them our puppy has spots. They said maybe he is a Dalmatian—and they ought to know because they used to have one!" Breathless, Morris went to the kitchen to forage for some food.

In a few minutes the Rumpels' next-door neighbours arrived.

"Let's have a look at this new dog of yours," said Mr. Murphy, putting on his glasses. But when they saw the puppy, the Murphys decided he was not a Dalmatian, after all. "He's sort of like a Samoyed," they said, "but not quite. He's got nice thick fur, though. What are you going to call him?"

"Snoopy," said Leah.

"Tramp," said Morris.

"I've got it!" exclaimed Quincy. "Snowflake! We can call him Snowflake because he's so snowy white. All except his spots, and they don't really show that much."

"He does look something like a big snowflake," said Leah, burying her face in the puppy's fur.

"I still like Tramp," grumbled Morris. "We have to vote."

"Dad, do we have to vote?" asked Quincy.

"Ask your mother."

"Mom?"

"It sounds fair," replied Mrs. Rumpel.

Mr. and Mrs. Rumpel abstained. Leah voted with Quincy, and Morris was outnumbered. The puppy was duly christened Snowflake.

"Can he sleep in our room tonight, Mom?" begged the girls.

"No," said their mother.

"Oh, Mom. The poor little thing!" moaned Quincy, hugging the puppy to her chest.

But Mrs. Rumpel was firm. "He might wet. He has to sleep downstairs. We'll make him a nice bed in the back hall."

They found an empty apple box in the basement and padded it with an old pair of Morris's pyjamas. Then they placed it in the back hall outside the kitchen and covered the floor around it with newspapers.

"Now," said Quincy, "we need some water in case he gets thirsty, an old shoe and a clock. Morris, where's that old sneaker you found on the beach?"

"I was saving it for a spare," said Morris, but in the end he produced the shoe. "It was getting too small for me, anyway," he admitted.

"What's the clock for?" asked Leah.

"To keep him company when he's all by himself away downstairs in the back hall." Quincy looked hard at her mother, but Mrs. Rumpel wasn't paying any attention. She was busy making a little pot of porridge.

"He might be hungry," she said.

When Snowflake was settled to everyone's satisfaction, the Rumpels went upstairs to bed. Leah was just falling asleep when Quincy hissed in her ear, "A radio! We forgot to leave a radio for him!"

"Huh?"

"Oh, never mind. Go back to sleep."

It was early the next morning when something woke Mrs. Rumpel. Outside it was still dark.

"I hear voices," she said, sitting bolt upright in bed. Beside her, Mr. Rumpel didn't stir.

She got up and opened the bedroom door. *Somebody was definitely talking downstairs*. Pulling on her dressing gown and taking the flashlight, she tiptoed down the steps.

As she crept through the kitchen, she heard, " ... with some chance of rain today. This has been the early, early morning weather report, brought to you by The Brolly Shoppe and Weather Wilma."

Mrs. Rumpel turned on the light. In the back hall a radio was playing, the apple box was empty, the newspapers were wet and there was a body in a sleeping bag on the floor.

It was Quincy. She was snoring gently. Snuggled against the back of her neck was a small bundle of white fur with black spots—also snoring.

Mrs. Rumpel turned off the radio. She put the wet papers in the garbage and spread fresh ones. Then she turned off the light and went back upstairs to bed. It was much too early to get up, she decided.

# 3

# The Arrival

"Hey, Quince, when do you suppose we'll get to go on TV?"

With Snowflake draped across her stomach asleep, Leah was lying on her bed eating an apple and watching Quincy do her homework.

Ever since the arrival of the Rumpel Rebounders, Leah and Quincy had given a lot of thought to the possibility (however faint) of helping their father advertise them on television.

"Ha. Soon, I hope." Quincy was sitting cross-legged on the floor stuffing polyester fill into a nylon stocking. An open French textbook was propped in front of her.

"Has Dad said anything about it?"

"No, but he might be getting close. Some of the rebounders are gone out of the living room, so he must be selling them. That means there might soon be enough money to advertise on TV. It's pretty expensive, I think."

"But he wouldn't have to pay us, so that would make it cheaper."

"I know," said Quincy. "That's why I'm going to join the band—so I could play a musical instrument. And I was thinking about Scottish dancing. Then I could do a sword dance. I might join the drama club, too. Don't worry, there'll be lots of stuff we can do on television. Maybe Snowflake can go on, even. He's so cute. Everybody would love to see him!"

"Maybe we could teach him to sit up and roll over!"

"Sure, and jump through a hoop! He'd look awfully cute doing that. I think I'll start training him."

Lifting the sleeping puppy off Leah's stomach, Quincy kissed him awake. Then she knelt on the floor and propped him up in front of her. Wobbling slightly, Snowflake stood facing her as she held her arms in a circle.

"See," she explained, "I start with my arms real low, so it's easy for him to jump over them. Come on, Snowflake. Jump!"

But Snowflake just blinked sleepily and slowly sagged to the floor. With his eyes shut tight and the tip of his pink tongue sticking out, he fell asleep.

"It's going to take time," said Quincy, putting him back on Leah's stomach. "We'll have to train him when he's more wide awake." And she returned to her polyester project.

"He wore himself out today, I guess," said Leah. "Mom says he chewed up the tea towel and spilled the garbage all over the floor. And he tore up the newspaper before Dad could read it … Maybe you could show how to make those stuffed dolls on TV."

"I don't think so. This one isn't doing too well." Quincy held up her lumpy nylon creation and studied it critically. The doll had a vague shape, with one plump leg and one skinny one. The stuffing in the arms had settled at the bottom, giving it hands like baseball mitts, while its head, due to a shortage of polyester fill, resembled a withered apple.

"Anyway, Gwen will probably want to do dolls. She's made three already," said Quincy.

"Yeah. Aunt Ida says they're good enough to put in the church bazaar, even."

"Huh!"

"I suppose Morris will want to be on, too."

"I don't think there'll be time for him. We'll have to spend some talking about how great the rebounders are. I wonder if we should do it in bilingual?"

Taking off her rose-tinted glasses, Quincy gave her widest smile. "Bonjour, everybody! Mon name est Quincy Rumpel! Ici est un Rumpel Rebounder ... "

"That sounds great. It's got class."

"I just might get a unicycle for my birthday and then I could ride that on TV, too." Making up her mind to talk to her father first thing in the morning about the advertising campaign, Quincy packed up her homework, shoved the doll under her bed and went downstairs for a snack.

But by the next morning, the Rumpels had something else to think about.

"Guess who's coming this weekend!" announced Mrs. Rumpel at breakfast.

"Wayne Gretzky!" shouted Morris, knocking over his orange juice.

"The Lippizan Stallions?" Leah looked hopeful.

"Could it be," Quincy smiled at her father and gave him a sly wink, "perhaps a TV producer?" Mr. Rumpel looked blank.

"Our first visitor from back east," proclaimed Mrs. Rumpel. "Aunt Fan!"

Aunt Fan was Mrs. Rumpel's aunt. In her younger days she had travelled abroad, mostly by train and boat. It was she who had brought them the cowbell from Switzerland. But airplanes rattled her, and lately she hadn't journeyed far from her home in Ontario. The Rumpels hadn't seen her since last Christmas.

"She phoned last night on the cheap rates," continued Mrs. Rumpel. "She's arriving Saturday, by plane."

"How long did you say she was staying?" Mr. Rumpel wanted to know.

"Ten days. She has to stay for ten days. It's some kind of special excursion rate."

"Where's she going to sleep?" wondered Leah.

"I thought we'd put her in Morris's room. He can sleep in Dad's office."

"Morris's room!" cried Quincy, aghast. "You can't put her in there!"

"What's the matter with my room?" demanded Morris.

When they first moved into their house in the summer, the Rumpels had been astonished to find that Morris's bedroom had black walls. It had been put on the priority list for repainting, but the Rumpels were running behind on their list. Morris, luckily, was very happy with his room. He had cheerfully decorated the walls with monster pictures. On the window sill sat his seaweed collection, two jars of dead bugs and a pale potato plant sprouting out of a mouldy potato.

It rained all that week and Mrs. Rumpel had to work at the umbrella shop, so it was not until Saturday morning that she got Morris moved into the cubbyhole under the stairs which Mr. Rumpel called his office. There was no door, and only a camp cot to sleep on. But on the plus side (said Morris), it was handy to the kitchen.

Saturday turned out to be sunny, so all the Rumpels went along for the ride to the airport. They were well on their way before Mr. Rumpel noticed Snowflake in the back seat.

"Where did he come from?" asked Mr. Rumpel.

"I guess he sort of sneaked in, Dad," replied Quincy. "Anyway, he won't be any trouble, I promise."

The Rumpels sped to the airport, only to find that Aunt Fan's plane had already unloaded. Aunt Fan herself was nowhere to be seen.

"Spread out, everybody, and look for her!" cried Mrs. Rumpel. "I'll search the washrooms." And she dashed away.

"Morris and I will check the bookstore," offered Mr. Rumpel.

"But I forget what she looks like," said Morris.

"Don't worry," his father told him. "She'll remember you. Now, you girls stick together and don't talk to anybody you don't know. We'll all meet back here in fifteen minutes."

"Gotcha, Dad!" said Quincy. "Shall we synchronize watches?"

"I don't think that's necessary," said Mr. Rumpel, scanning the bookshelves.

Leah and Quincy took off at once, proceeding to inspect all the likely looking elderly ladies. "Aunt Fan might not recognize me now that I have my ears pierced," said Quincy, as they circled the main terminal.

They ended up back at the bookstore, where their father and Morris were still browsing. "Should we go downstairs and look?" asked Quincy.

"Good idea," replied Mr. Rumpel absently. He seemed to be absorbed in a book called, "New Careers From Old Hobbies."

As the two girls rode down the escalator, they noticed a majestic figure in a flowing purple cape darting around below. "There she is! I remember that cape!" cried Quincy.

As they stepped off the escalator, the purple cape suddenly whirled around and its occupant crashed into them.

"My stars and garters!" exclaimed Aunt Fan. "If it isn't little Quincy and Leah!" Enveloping them in the woolly folds of her vast cape, she hugged them. "My dear children, the most dreadful thing has happened." Aunt Fan's luggage, it seemed, was lost. She feared it might even have gone back to Toronto. "I knew I should have taken the train," she said.

Just then she noticed two airline pilots striding past carrying their flight bags. Flanked by Leah and Quincy, she sailed over to them. "Pardon me, my good men, but I wonder if you might have seen my luggage? It's a matched set of red vinyl, brand new, with a tote bag full of maple syrup."

"Have you looked over there under that sign, madam?" suggested one of the pilots, pointing to a large illuminated sign that said LUGGAGE PICKUP.

Squinting her eyes, Aunt Fan peered around her. "Of course, how stupid of me!" she exclaimed. But after the men had gone, she confided to Leah and Quincy, "I still don't see any sign."

"Maybe you should get glasses, Aunt Fan," said Quincy.

"Oh, I've got glasses. But I only wear them when I really need them."

The two girls led Aunt Fan over to the luggage pickup. The area was deserted, and the conveyor belt was empty except for three red vinyl suitcases and a matching tote, riding around in solitary splendour.

"There they are!" cried Aunt Fan. "I hope the syrup hasn't leaked."

"I'll get them for you, Auntie!" Lunging forward, Quincy made a grab for the suitcases. But they were hooked together by the strap of the tote. The whole cluster trundled on past and eventually disappeared behind the dangling flaps of a rubber curtain.

Quincy waited. In a few minutes the red ensemble came tottering toward them again. This time Quincy was ready. Pouncing onto the moving belt, she wiggled along on her stomach until she reached the luggage. The last Aunt Fan and Leah saw of her, Quincy was fumbling with the tote strap. Then she slowly vanished behind the rubber flaps.

Leah screamed and Aunt Fan fainted. At that moment, Mr. and Mrs. Rumpel and Morris stepped off the escalator.

Hearing the scream, Mrs. Rumpel cried, "That's Leah!"

They found Aunt Fan stretched out on the floor, swathed in her cape and with the toes of her purple boots pointing skyward. A little crowd had gathered around her. As they hovered nervously, someone fanned her with her purple velvet hat.

Meanwhile, as Leah mumbled incoherently and pointed to the conveyor belt and the rubber flaps, Quincy herself suddenly came into view at the other end.

Sitting calmly among Aunt Fan's red suitcases, she was holding the tote on her lap.

"Hi, Mom! Hi, Dad!" she cried, waving.

Someone stopped the moving belt, and Quincy and the luggage were plucked off. Aunt Fan was revived and set on her feet again, apparently none the worse.

"Are you sure you're all right?" Mrs. Rumpel asked her as they squeezed into the front seat of the station wagon.

"Of course I'm all right. I faint quite often when I'm wearing these boots. I am worried about that poor child, though!" Aunt Fan turned around to look at Quincy. "Just look how pale she is!" she cried, peering into Snowflake's earnest white face.

Aunt Fan still didn't have her glasses on.

# 4

# Frozen Chickens
# and Other Trials

"I hope you won't hate Morris's room too much," said Quincy, carrying a red suitcase upstairs.

Aunt Fan gazed around her new quarters smiling happily. She took off her purple velvet hat, knocking it against several small plastic skeletons dangling from the ceiling and setting them swinging. Quincy held her breath.

"It looks just fine, dear," said Aunt Fan, plunking the hat down on the dresser on top of Morris's stuffed skunk.

Shrugging, Quincy went down to the kitchen where she found her mother muttering to herself as she whacked something against the edge of the sink.

"Forget to thaw out the chicken again, Mom?" asked Quincy, helping herself to a handful of soda crackers.

"Frozen chickens! Frozen chickens!"

Munching her crackers, Quincy sat at the table reading the funnies, while Mrs. Rumpel tried vainly to pry apart the legs of the chicken. Neither of them heard Aunt Fan shuffle into the kitchen in her knitted purple slippers. Staggering over to a chair, she collapsed onto it.

Aunt Fan looked stunned as she peered out from behind a pair of large, rhinestone-trimmed glasses with purple frames.

"That boy's room! There are pictures of *creatures* all over the walls," she whispered hoarsely. "With sticky blood!"

"We know," said Mrs. Rumpel.

"And little skeletons dangling from the ceiling!"

"Our Morris is thinking of being a doctor when he grows up," Mrs. Rumpel said proudly. Leaving the chicken to soak in the sink, she put the kettle on for tea.

"Would you like to sleep downstairs on the chesterfield, Auntie? We could clear it off," she added.

After a cup of hot tea, Aunt Fan felt better. "I'll be all right in Morris's room, dear. It's nice and near the bathroom. Anyway, you have an awful lot of boxes in the living room. What is Harvey collecting now?"

"That's our new business," Quincy told her. "Rumpel Rebounders! Maybe someday we'll even advertise on TV."

Supper was late that night, starting and finishing. Aunt Fan, full of news from back east about various Twistles and their ailments and achievements, chatted on and on. It wasn't until the next morning that Quincy got a chance to talk to her father.

"When do you think we can do it, Dad? Advertise on TV, I mean."

"TV?" said Mr. Rumpel. "There's no money to spare for that sort of thing right now."

"Well," said Quincy, "at least that will give us time to get practised up. Which do you think would be best—me riding a unicycle or me doing a sword dance?"

"I didn't know you could do either," said her father.

"I can't yet. But I could learn to ride a unicycle if I had one. And I do have a birthday coming up." Quincy glanced coyly at her father, but he was busy spreading marmalade on his toast.

"Where's Morris?" asked Mr. Rumpel. "And has anybody seen Aunt Fan this morning?"

"Morris isn't hungry. He says he couldn't sleep, so he snacked on crackers and cheese all night," said Quincy.

At that moment Aunt Fan tottered into the kitchen. She was wearing a long purple robe decorated with several large golden dragons. Almost unnoticed in her white hair was a small plastic skeleton.

"Good morning, Auntie," said Mrs. Rumpel, handing her a glass of orange juice. "How did you sleep?"

"*They glowed*," quavered Aunt Fan. "*Those things glowed all night*!"

"I told you not to put her in Morris's room," said Quincy, making herself a piece of French toast.

"And I heard a clock strike *thirteen*!"

"It always does that after it strikes twelve," Quincy told her. "Ever since Dad fixed it."

Morris was detailed to remove his skeletons and monsters. "That's okay," he said. "I couldn't sleep very well without them, anyway." He placed them lovingly all around Mr. Rumpel's office, together with his seaweed collection, bottled bugs and potato plant. The stuffed skunk he set on the fireplace mantel in the living room for safekeeping.

From then on, both he and Aunt Fan slept better.

"Where's your sister?" Mrs. Rumpel asked Leah a few days later.

"She stayed at school to join the band." Swinging open the refrigerator door, Leah stood contemplating the contents inside.

"Here, have an apple," said her mother. "And you and Morris can take Snowflake for his walk. But be sure and keep him on the leash."

"We have to. He's starting to chase cars already."

Snowflake, never small to begin with, was growing rapidly. His coat was long and his feet large. He was still basically white, except for his seven spots, which seemed to be getting bigger and blacker. He didn't look quite so much like a snowflake any more.

If he didn't get exercised every day, Snowflake dug gigantic holes in the backyard. Twice he had tunnelled under the fence to visit the Murphys.

By the time Leah and Morris returned from walking him that day, supper was ready but Quincy still wasn't home. They were just going to start without her when she burst in the front door lugging a large instrument case. She was followed by Gwen, who carried a small one.

"Guess what!" cried Quincy. "We get to keep our instruments all weekend! Can Gwen stay for supper so we can practise after?"

"Help yourselves," said Mrs. Rumpel.

"Something smells delectable," said Gwen, crinkling up her nose.

"It's zucchini stew," Morris told her, reaching for a second helping. "It's yucky."

Quincy was busy opening her black case. "Isn't it beautiful?" she cried, holding up a brass trombone, somewhat battered and covered in fingerprints. "We're supposed to learn 'Mary Had a Little Lamb' for Monday."

"How did she have it, fried?" snorted Morris with his mouth full.

Quincy raised the instrument to her lips and let go with several squawks. "It's going to take a little practice," she said. "But doesn't it sound cool? And look how far it slides out! Do you want to see my spit valve?"

"Oh, gross!" groaned Leah.

"All the Twistles are musical," said Aunt Fan. "Your cousin Gertie took harp lessons once. Her teacher said she had a natural talent for it and was the best pupil he'd ever had."

"Is she a famous harpist now?" asked Quincy.

"She might have been, but she ran away with a bell-ringer and now she has six children. They all ring bells, except the baby, of course, but even he has bells on his rattle ... "

"What instrument are you learning, Gwen?" asked Mrs. Rumpel when Aunt Fan paused for a drink of coffee.

"The flute. I might even be a professional flautist someday. You know, like Zamfir."

"Well, as long as Quincy doesn't have plans to become a professional trombonist ... " said Mr. Rumpel. "I don't think we could handle ten years of tromboning."

"Harvey, you mustn't discourage the child!" protested Aunt Fan.

46

"It's all right, Aunt Fan," said Quincy. "I'm only taking it so I can do it when we go on TV. I've got lots of other things to be when I grow up. Probably I'll be a dog trainer for seeing eye dogs. I'm going to practise on Snowflake and teach him tricks."

"You should teach him not to chase cars," said Morris. "He chased another one today and, boy, did the driver ever get mad."

"Ah-*ha*! A car chaser, is he?" said Aunt Fan. "Cousin Lester had a car chaser once, and he soon trained him out of it."

"How?" chorused the Rumpels.

"With a pail of cold water. Cousin Lester drove past the dog, and when he ran out after the car, Lester threw a pail of water on him. Leroy never chased another car."

"Maybe we should try it," said Mrs. Rumpel.

"Well, if you're going to try the water treatment, you'd better do it early in the morning before there's any traffic," said Mr. Rumpel.

It was barely daylight the next morning when the little group gathered in the chilly air on the curb in front of Number 57. Aunt Fan, in her dragon dressing gown, had a firm grip on Snowflake's collar. Snowflake himself kept sagging against her knees and dozing off. Behind them,

Leah and Morris stood shivering in their ski jackets and pyjamas. Quincy, in her orange ski sweater and a pair of jeans, got in the front seat of the station wagon beside her mother. She held a pail of cold water balanced on her knees.

"You'd better drive around the block once first," Aunt Fan told them, "so Snowflake won't recognize you. Then when you come driving past, I'll release him."

"Gotcha!" said Quincy. "And that's when I throw the water!"

"Quincy gets to do all the fun part," complained Morris, as his mother put the car in gear and took off down the street. Aunt Fan tightened her grip on Snowflake.

In a few minutes the station wagon appeared again around the corner and came toward the little group standing on the curb.

"Here they come!" shouted Morris. "Wake up, Snowflake!"

Snowflake looked around sleepily as the car approached.

"NOW!" cried Aunt Fan, letting go of his collar.

"YAHOOO!" yelled Quincy, heaving both water and pail out the window.

The water caught Aunt Fan squarely in the face, while the pail went clattering down the street. Snowflake took off after it, yelping happily.

As Mrs. Rumpel screeched to a stop, the Murphys suddenly appeared at their bedroom window. Mr. Murphy had on a red flannel nightshirt and Mrs. Murphy's hair was in curlers. They stared out the window, trying to figure out what was going on.

"I guess Snowflake didn't feel like chasing cars today," said Quincy. "Maybe it was too early for him."

"I think it was too early for all of us," said her mother, as she helped a dripping-wet Aunt Fan back into the house.

After the last class on Monday, Quincy and Gwen hurried to the music room for band practice. "Oh, boy," said Quincy, "I can hardly wait! I've been practising all weekend! Aunt Fan said my version of 'Mary Had a Little Lamb' is so good that I don't need to practise any more. I hope Mr. Fife asks me to do a solo. I know every note!"

But the band teacher began the lesson by talking and writing scales on the blackboard. He talked on and on, and soon Quincy was squirming in her seat. "B-o-r-i-n-g!" she mouthed at Gwen. If old Fife kept on talking, there wouldn't be any time left for her to do a solo.

Yawning, she clasped her hands behind her head and leaned back. Something poked her in the shoulder. But when she turned around to glare at Freddie Twikenham, who sat behind her, Freddie was just sitting behind his tuba, gazing out the window.

This is dullsville, for sure, thought Quincy. I could really liven things up if I could do my solo! And she began waving her arm in the air.

"Miss Rumpel, would you please put your hand down," said Mr. Fife. "I'm not finished talking yet. And it wouldn't hurt you to take a few notes like some of the others."

Sighing loudly, Quincy rolled her eyes at Gwen, who shrugged her shoulders and kept on writing.

Taking her eraser out of her jeans pocket, Quincy began flipping it across her desk with the end of a pencil.

Suddenly the eraser took off over her shoulder and disappeared. Quincy looked around her and on the floor behind, but didn't see it anywhere. "It's in there," Gwen whispered, pointing to Freddie's tuba.

Reaching behind, Quincy stuck her arm inside the cavernous open end. She groped around, but felt nothing. Her eraser was lost somewhere in the dark, nethermost regions of the big brass instrument.

Quincy shoved her arm in farther, right up to her armpit. By this time most of the class were watching her in silent fascination, as Mr. Fife, all unknowing, continued to write on the blackboard. Suddenly Quincy felt her fingers triumphantly close around the small square rubber. But when she tried to pull it out, her arm wouldn't come.

"Psssst! Gwen!" hissed Quincy. "I'm stuck!" But Gwen took one look and pretended not to hear.

As Quincy tugged at her arm, Freddie tightened his grip. "Get your arm outta my tuba!" he whispered crossly, giving it a yank.

"YEEEEOW!"

Laying down his chalk, Mr. Fife turned around. "And what's the matter now, Miss Rumpel?" he sighed.

"My eraser, sir," gasped Quincy. "It fell in Freddie's tuba, and now my arm's stuck." Around her, the other kids were snickering and standing up to get a better view.

Her face beet-red, Quincy gave one final heave. Suddenly there was a sound like a cork coming out of a bottle, and out popped her arm.

Grinning with relief, Quincy waved the eraser over her head in triumph, and everyone cheered.

"All right, people!" said Mr. Fife. "Perhaps we can continue, if Miss Rumpel is quite finished." Quincy nodded.

While Freddie checked his tuba for damage, the music lesson was resumed. But no one got to play a solo.

At last Aunt Fan's visit was over. After breakfast, her luggage was securely locked and loaded in the back of the station wagon.

"We'd better hurry," said Mr. Rumpel. "We don't want to miss that plane." And he went out to start the motor. He would be driving Aunt Fan to the airport alone. Mrs. Rumpel had to work and the children had to go to school.

Aunt Fan, with a map of Canada tucked into her purse in case the pilot mislaid his, was dressed and ready well ahead of time. She stood at the front door and swept each of the Rumpels into the folds of her woolly cape as she hugged them goodbye. Then, with tears in her eyes, she opened the door. "Sayonara!" she called, giving a brave little wave.

Suddenly Mrs. Rumpel cried, "Auntie! You've still got your slippers on!"

Opening her purse, Aunt Fan took out her rhinestone-trimmed glasses and put them on. "Oh, my stars and garters!" she cried, staring down at her feet in disbelief.

While Mr. Rumpel fidgeted in the car, Quincy, Leah and Morris were sent to look for Aunt Fan's boots.

They eventually found one under Morris's bed, but not the other. It didn't turn up until weeks later when Quincy was cleaning out Snowflake's apple box.

Tucked in a corner under Morris's pyjamas she found the shredded remains of a purple boot, well chewed.

# 5

# Colour-Coded, et Cetera

As Quincy, Leah and Gwen scuffed home from school, Quincy kicked at a pile of fallen autumn leaves and sent them flying. "I've been thinking about getting colour-coded," she said.

"What's that?" Leah wanted to know.

"It's just colour-coded, that's all. Everybody knows what it is."

"I never heard you talk about it before."

"She just means finding out her right colours," Gwen explained. "Like, if you're a spring or summer person."

"A *what* person?"

"If we're going on TV soon, I should wear the right colours, et cetera, et cetera. It could make a lot of difference in the impression I make. Hey, look at all the chestnuts!" Suddenly Quincy stopped and began to stuff her pockets with the shiny nuts.

"I saw this ad," she went on, hopping around as she scooped them up, "and they'll tell you everything for twelve dollars. What colour of lipstick and everything."

Stooping to gather some chestnuts, Leah said, "But you've never even worn lip gloss. You don't even use deodorant yet."

"I'm gonna start soon. I just hope I'm an autumn person. Then maybe I'd get to wear this chestnut colour. I just love it."

"Anyway, where are you going to get twelve dollars?" Leah wanted to know.

Quincy looked thoughtful. "Maybe I could make chestnut necklaces and sell them."

"Maybe you could borrow the money from Morris again," suggested her sister.

"Ha!" laughed Gwen. "Remember when you had to pay Morris back for your Save-the-Whales T-Shirt?"

"Do I!" groaned Quincy. "I never worked so hard in all my life. I'll never borrow money from that little tightwad again!"

"Where is he, by the way?" asked Gwen, noticing for the first time that Morris wasn't with them.

"He has a friend now, thank goodness," replied Quincy. "Chucky. Sometimes he goes over to his house to play."

"Say, I've got an idea," said Gwen. "About colour coding et cetera. There must be lots of stuff at the library. You know, magazines and books. About fashion and style.''

''I know all about style. I just want to see if I'm an autumn person.''

''You could do with some help with your style, too.'' Gwen looked critically at her cousin. ''Nobody wears feather earrings any more, you know.''

''But I love them!''

''Quincy wants suspender pants,'' said Leah. ''They're stylish.''

''That's what I mean!'' cried Gwen in exasperation. ''She's the wrong shape for suspender pants. Now, if it were me, it would be different.''

''I don't care. I still want some. Wouldn't they look great on TV if I was riding a unicycle? Especially if they were colour-coded! Come on, we may as well go to the library and look at stuff.''

The next morning, Mrs. Rumpel was surprised to find a stack of fashion and glamour magazines spilling out from under Quincy's bed.

A few days later a brand-new, giant-sized bottle of deodorant suddenly appeared on the dresser. Securely sealed in its tight plastic container, it sat there all week gathering dust.

Among the many things Quincy had learned while poring over the magazines was that she was not, after all, an autumn person. She was spring. So was Leah. Gwen was summer.

"And guess who's autumn?" Quincy declared in disgust. "Morris. That's who!"

"He can't help it if he has brown eyes," said Leah. "When are you going to use your new d.o.?"

"Pretty soon now. I'm almost ready."

One morning soon after, as the Rumpels milled about in the kitchen getting their breakfasts, Mr. Rumpel asked, "Where's Quincy?"

"She's still getting ready," replied Leah, spreading peanut butter on a piece of toast.

"There's no onion bagels and there's no Crunchie Munchies," grumbled Morris, staring bleakly into the refrigerator. "If I don't get more food I'm going to be a midget all my life … "

"Have an egg," said his mother, pressing her nose to the window pane. "Oh, darn," she cried, "it's starting to rain! Uncle George will be phoning any minute now to call me in to work."

"I thought you liked working," said Leah.

"I did, at first. But I never thought it would rain so much. I don't even have time to shop for birdseed!"

One of Mr. Rumpel's first projects when they moved into their house had been to design, construct and install a large wooden bird feeder outside the kitchen window. "It will be educational for the children and interesting for everybody," he had said, describing the different kinds of birds they would be seeing. To protect them from the rain, he had fashioned a Chinese pagoda-style roof, complete with little shell wind-chimes (made by Quincy) at the corners. However, though the feeder was kept filled with a gourmet mixture of wild birdseed, the only birds to visit so far were sparrows. These came in great flocks and ate steadily all day.

"Don't tell me we're out of birdseed again," groaned Mr. Rumpel, gloomily cracking his boiled egg. "Those darn birds are eating up all our profits!"

"Oh, Harvey," said his wife, "it's not as bad as all that!"

Suddenly the conversation was interrupted by the honk of a trombone, and Quincy appeared in the doorway. Removing the trombone from her glossy pink lips with a flourish, she greeted her family.

"Introducing ... the All-New Quincy Rumpel! Here she is, folks—the TV personality of the year! Brought to you live by the one and only Rumpel Rebounders!"

Behind her pink glasses, Quincy's blue eyes were outlined in black kohl eyeliner. Her hair jutted out over her forehead like an overhanging eave, held in position by generous amounts of gel. Large pink plastic loop earrings dangled from her ears, and her fingernails glowed with fluorescent polish to match her lips. She wore her dog-paw print blouse, her maroon cords, and a pair of new and splendid red suspenders.

Mrs. Rumpel gasped.

Quincy flapped her arms. "I've got deodorant on, too," she said proudly.

"How did you finance all this finery?" asked her mother.

"I saved some of my allowance, and I sold Mrs. Murphy six chestnut necklaces."

"How on earth is she going to wear six chestnut necklaces?"

"Oh, she's not going to wear them. She's going to hang them in her closets to keep the spiders away, she says. So, Dad, I'm ready to go on TV any time you're ready. Just say the magic word!"

"Good grief!" said Mr. Rumpel.

# 6

# The Present

Clad in her bedroom slippers and a pair of Quincy's old jogging pants, Mrs. Rumpel was in the living room trying to twirl a hula hoop about her waist.

"I used to be good at this," she said to Quincy. "Why can't I do it any more?"

"Because your hips aren't swivelling, Mom. You've got to really move 'em."

Mrs. Rumpel swivelled desperately, but the hula hoop kept sliding down her legs to settle around her ankles. "I'm in terrible shape," groaned Mrs. Rumpel.

"No, you aren't, Mom. You should see Freddie Twikenham's mother! You could probably even go on TV with us, if necessary. Anyway, you've got great teeth."

"All the Twistles have good teeth," panted Mrs. Rumpel. "Oh, by the way, a parcel came for you today from Grandma Twistle. Probably a birthday present. She always sends them early."

"Oh, boy! Where is it?"

"Upstairs. Don't you want to keep it for your birthday?"

"No. I need cheering up now. Miss Dingwall separated Gwen and me today. She said Gwen wasn't having a good influence on me, but I was having a questionable influence on her! How do you like that? Where's my present?"

"In the linen cupboard."

Quincy took the stairs two at a time. Good old Grandma Twistle! One never knew what she would send. For *her* twelfth birthday, Gwen had received a long white satin nightgown trimmed with red rosebuds.

Quickly locating the parcel under the hot water bottle, Quincy carried it carefully downstairs. "It sort of thuds," she reported, tilting it back and forth. "And it's sort of heavy."

"Maybe it's a giant box of chocolates," suggested Leah, who was just coming in the front door.

"Do you suppose it could be a chest expander? Boy, would I love a chest expander!"

"Why don't you open it and find out?" asked Mrs. Rumpel.

Giving the parcel one last shake, Quincy started peeling off layers of brown paper. "It must be something special," she said, "with all this wrapping." At last she came to a box covered in birthday paper. "Oh, boy! Horses! My favourite paper!"

Underneath that was a flowered box. "Ta-*da*!" cried Quincy, flinging off the lid.

"What is it? chorused Mrs. Rumpel and Leah, hanging over Quincy's shoulder.

"I'm not sure. It's green, and rubbery … "

"Maybe it's a new shower curtain," said Leah.

Gingerly, Quincy lifted her present out of its tissue-paper nest. Promptly unfolding itself, it cascaded to the floor.

"It's a poncho," cried Quincy in dismay. "It's a horrible, giant-sized, green rubber poncho!"

"So it is," said Mrs. Rumpel. She couldn't think of anything else to say.

With her glasses stuck up in her hair, Quincy was sitting on the bench in the front hall mournfully blowing her trombone. Suddenly Morris burst in clutching Snowflake's empty collar. It was still attached to the leash.

"Guess what," he cried. "Snowflake's gone!"

"Gone? What do you mean, gone?"

"Like I said. Leah and me took him out for a walk and he ran away."

"You let him off the leash? You know you're not supposed to let him off the leash!"

"We only did it for a minute. We wanted to see if he could heel yet. We couldn't undo the snap, so we took his collar right off, and then he ran away."

Suddenly Morris noticed the poncho lying like some deflated green monster on the floor. "What's that?" he cried.

"Never mind. Come on, we've got to find Snowflake!" Grabbing Morris by the hand, Quincy dragged him to the door. "Now show me where you lost him."

"I didn't say we lost him. I said he's gone. He's right over there." Morris pointed across the street. "He just won't come home."

Pulling her glasses down, Quincy peered across to where Snowflake stood smelling something in an empty lot. Behind him some bushes were quivering. It was Leah. Suddenly she made a grab for him, but Snowflake slipped out of her grasp and bolted away.

"Come back here, you dumb dog!" yelled Leah.

Waving the leash and collar, Quincy ran across the road. "Snowflake, come!" she hollered.

At the sound of her voice, Snowflake stopped in his tracks, tail wagging joyfully. "RUFF! RUFF!" he barked.

"Come on, Snowflake, there's a good dog." Eyes narrowed, Quincy stalked through the long wet grass ... *Join Quincy Rumpel on safari in deepest Africa as she hunts the wily wildebeest, armed only with her video camera and recorder ...*

As Quincy advanced, Snowflake stood motionless, watching her. Then, just as she reached for him, the dog bounded playfully away.

"Darn dog!" said Quincy.

"Here comes Mom," announced Morris, as Mrs. Rumpel came running down the front steps clutching a wad of hamburger meat.

"Give me that leash," she ordered. "I know how to catch him."

With the leash and collar hidden behind her back, she moved toward Snowflake. "Here, Snowflake. Good doggie. Come and get this yummy meat," coaxed Mrs. Rumpel.

Snowflake sat down and watched her suspiciously.

"He doesn't know her because she's wearing Quincy's pants," said Leah.

Smacking her lips and holding the hamburger enticingly out in front of her, Mrs. Rumpel continued her advance.

Suddenly Snowflake leaped forward, gulped the meat and retreated behind some bushes.

"That does it!" declared Mrs. Rumpel. "We're not wasting any more time on that dog. Children, come on home!" And she stomped off over the soggy lot, her baggy jogging pants billowing out with every step.

Quincy searched the empty lot one more time, but there was no trace of Snowflake.

"He's gone for sure this time," sobbed Leah, as they all trailed home.

"We'll never see Snowflake again!" moaned Morris.

"Who left the front door open?" asked Mrs. Rumpel, as they climbed the wooden front steps of their house.

"You must have, Mom," said Quincy. "You were the last one out."

As Mrs. Rumpel paused on the verandah to take off her wet slippers, Morris charged past on his way to the kitchen.

"Hey! Here's Snowflake!" he cried. "Right here in the house!"

"Where? Where?" cried Quincy and Leah, rushing inside.

Snowflake was lying on the chesterfield in the living room, happily chewing the hula hoop.

"Oh, good dog!" cried Quincy, running over to him and throwing her arms around him. "Morris, go and get him a treat!"

"A treat? What kind of a treat?"

"Something good. Maybe some more of that hamburger meat. He liked that. I read in a dog training book that they're supposed to get an instant reward when they do something good.''

"What has he done that's good?'' demanded Mrs. Rumpel, wiping dog drool off the hula hoop.

"He did come home, Mom,'' said Leah, hugging Snowflake. "I think that's pretty good.''

Just then Morris's voice rang out shrilly from the kitchen. "There's no hamburger here!''

"Yes, there is,'' answered Mrs. Rumpel. "There's a whole package of it on the counter.''

"There's only some chewed-up paper on the floor. What else will I bring him? A muffin?''

"What else?'' cried Mrs. Rumpel. "Nothing else, that's what! That dog just ate our supper!''

# 7

# Red Suspenders

"Did you see Mom this morning?" asked Leah. "She's bought herself some exercise tights and jogging shoes. She's downstairs working out on the rebounder, and it's only seven o'clock!"

"Yeah, I know. She's been trying to get in shape. The trouble is, she doesn't look any different yet." Quincy was sitting cross-legged on the bed in her green-striped pyjamas, with Snowflake beside her. She was examining her earring collection—all three pairs.

"Which do you think look best—my dog ones, my feather ones or my new pink plastic hoops?" she asked.

"The pink plastic hoops, I guess. I wish my ears were pierced ... "

"Well, I tried. But you wouldn't let me. Do you want me to try again?"

"Are you crazy?" Shuddering at the memory of that day in the summer when Quincy had chased her around the house with a sterilized needle and a cork, Leah clapped her hands firmly over her ears. "Anyway, how come you're fussing about your earrings? You're only going to school."

"I'm going to Morris's soccer practice afterwards. I think he needs some support."

"Wow! That's a change!"

"Yes, Desmond says a team's support is very important."

"Who's Desmond?"

"Morris's soccer coach. Boy, is he ever a hunk! And his glasses have stainless-steel frames just like mine."

"Has he noticed you yet?"

"I think so. At the last practice, at half-time when they were standing around eating their oranges, I went right over and pulled up Morris's socks. I'm sure he noticed me."

That morning at breakfast Morris sneezed twice. "I hope you're not coming down with a cold," said his mother. "Maybe you'd better not go to soccer practice today."

"I have to go. There's a big game coming up," replied Morris. "Anyway, I'm all right."

"Sure, he's all right!" said Quincy. "The fresh air will be good for him."

Mrs. Rumpel looked at Quincy, dressed in her dog-paw print blouse, her good cords and her new red suspenders. She had on her pink plastic earrings, and there were dark smudges around her eyes.

"What's the matter? Why are you looking at me like that?" asked Quincy, batting her eyelashes at her mother. This left even more dark smudges.

"Nothing, I guess," said Mrs. Rumpel. "It's just your … eyes. What have you done to them?"

"I borrowed some of your new mascara. I didn't think you'd mind. Gwen says I've got invisible eyelashes."

"I think you'd better wash that off and try again. Next time, just use a little bit," advised Mrs. Rumpel. "Is there something special going on today?"

"No, nothing special." Quincy's voice squeaked as she said it.

"Only Morris's soccer practice," snickered Leah.

"If you're coming to my soccer practice again," said Morris, glaring at Quincy, "stay away from me! AND LEAVE MY SOCKS ALONE!"

After breakfast Quincy went up to the bathroom and dabbed at her eyes with a wet washcloth. "I sure hate to take it all off," she told Leah. "It took me hours to put it on."

"Don't worry," Leah told her. "It's still on. But don't let Mom see you."

As it happened, Mrs. Rumpel was busy hula-hooping in the living room when they left and just blew them three kisses.

"I'm afraid Mom is overdoing it," said Leah as they ran down the front steps. "She's going to burn herself out before she's forty."

"I think she's hoping to go on TV with us. I wish Dad would hurry up and put us on before I grow any more. I'm practically taller than Desmond already."

"Well, if we're going on TV for sure, we'd better figure out what we're going to do pretty soon. Mom says we can't take Scottish dancing lessons this year, so you won't be doing a sword dance. And your trombone playing isn't exactly … "

"I don't think the trombone is such a hot instrument, anyway," said Quincy, who had lost interest in the band since the tuba incident. "Anyway, I still might get a unicycle for my birthday, and that's only the day after Halloween."

"What if you don't get one? Snowflake isn't shaping up too well as a trick dog, either."

"Don't worry. I'll think of something."

As they hurried down Tulip Street, they could see Gwen standing out in front of her house. "What kept you so long?" she asked. "Where's Morris?"

"He went on ahead because Quincy was taking so long getting ready," replied Leah. "How do you like her all spiffied up?"

Quincy blinked her eyes at her cousin. "Well, it's sort of an improvement, I guess," said Gwen. "What's the occasion?"

"Nothing," answered Quincy.

"She's going to Morris's soccer practice after school," said Leah.

"I thought you didn't like soccer," Gwen said to Quincy.

"I just thought I'd go, is all. Morris needs support."

"His coach is a real hunk, Quincy says," piped up Leah.

"Oh?" said Gwen, fluffing up her hair. "Actually, I'm quite fond of soccer, myself. Maybe I'll go with you."

"You don't need to," muttered Quincy.

"After all," said Gwen, "Morris is my cousin. I'm coming, too."

After school the three girls hurried over to the playing field. Despite a cool wind blowing off the sea, Quincy carried her jacket, not wanting to cover up her red suspenders.

As they approached the field, they saw that the soccer practice was already in progress. "Hey, who's that blowing the whistle?" asked Quincy, coming to a sudden halt.

"It's a girl," replied Leah, squinting.

"That's Sandy Brickleback, the girl coach," said Gwen, who knew almost everybody. "She's in high school."

"Which one is Desmond?" Leah wanted to know.

Quincy peered out over the soccer field. At last she said, "Desmond isn't here. He's not here at all! And after I went to all this trouble ... I'm going home!" And she stomped off, her pink earrings flapping and the buckles on her red suspenders gleaming in the fall sunshine.

"Don't you want to support Morris's team?" yelled Leah, running after her.

Quincy didn't answer.

After checking out the soccer field one last time, Gwen turned and followed the others. "Hey, wait for me," she called.

Catching up with Quincy, Leah said, "Don't worry. The big game is on Saturday. Desmond will probably be there then."

"I suppose so," said Quincy, her spirits rising slightly.

"I'm coming with you," said Gwen. "What should I wear?"

"Gee, it doesn't matter what you wear to a soccer game," answered Quincy grumpily.

"*You're* all dressed up." Gwen patted her blonde hair. "I think I'll wear my white fur-trimmed parka and my black stirrup pants."

"Huh."

"Well, see you tomorrow," said Gwen when they reached her house. "Mummy's out and I have to make a quiche for supper tonight."

"Sometimes Gwen gives me a pain," Quincy said to Leah, as the two girls meandered on down Tulip Street.

"I'll bet you could make a quiche if you tried," said Leah, scuffing through a pile of leaves.

Suddenly Quincy stopped and pointed down the street. "Hey, the car's out in front. Dad was supposed to be out making deliveries today. I wonder what's up?"

When the two girls arrived home, the house was unusually quiet. On the floor in the living room lay Mrs. Rumpel's hula hoop.

"Mom!" hollered Quincy.

"Sssshhh!" Mr. Rumpel came tiptoeing down the stairs. "Your mother is resting. She has had a little accident. She's upstairs now on the bed, but she's pretty groggy. Don't be noisy when you go up."

Galloping up the stairs, Quincy and Leah rushed into their parents' bedroom.

Her eyes closed and a hot-water bottle on her head, Mrs. Rumpel lay on top of the bedspread in her new blue exercise tights and her new pink joggers.

"Mom has such cute little feet," said Quincy.

Slowly, Mrs. Rumpel opened one eye. "My poor babies!" she cried, holding out her arms.

"Mom! You can talk!" exclaimed Quincy, diving onto the bed and nearly smothering her mother with a bear-hug, while Leah sobbed happily as she straightened the hot-water bottle.

"Ta-*da*!" proclaimed Mr. Rumpel, appearing in the doorway with a tray. "Coffee time!" On the tray were two mugs of coffee, a plate of donuts and, in a little vase, the last rose from the Rumpels' rose bush. All this was neatly arranged on a tea towel from the kitchen.

"Oh, Harvey!" cried Mrs. Rumpel, quite overcome.

While she sipped her coffee and everybody munched donuts, she explained what had happened. "I just bounced too high while I was twirling my hula hoop, and I hit my head on the chandelier."

"You mean you were actually bouncing on the rebounder and twirling the hoop at the same time?" asked Quincy, aghast. "*Under the chandelier*?"

Mrs. Rumpel nodded guiltily and took another sip of coffee.

"It was lucky your father happened to come home just then to pick up some rebounders," said Mrs. Rumpel. "Or I might still be lying there."

"Someday we'll have to move that darn chandelier!" Mr. Rumpel reached for another donut. He had found his beloved wife out cold on the living-room floor, and had immediately called the doctor. Cold compresses had been prescribed. "So then I thought of putting ice cubes in the hot-water bottle," he finished proudly.

"I saw stars and garters," Mrs. Rumpel told them. "I felt my head whack on the chandelier and then I actually saw stars and garters!"

"Just like Aunt Fan!" marvelled Leah.

Suddenly Quincy spoke up. "Do you think you could get really good at it?" she asked her mother. "I mean, twirling and bouncing at the same time? Maybe you could do it on TV!"

Mr. Rumpel looked puzzled. "TV? Are you going on TV?"

"She might be, Dad. If she could learn to do something, that is. Don't you remember? You said you might let us help you advertise Rumpel Rebounders on TV!"

"If I did, I don't know what I was thinking of. Anyway, things are a little slow just now. We won't be doing much of anything for a while."

"But when you do, can we be on it?" persisted Quincy. "At least some of us. We could do all sorts of things and save you lots of money."

"Well, maybe. *If* I ever do it."

"Don't count on me," said Mrs. Rumpel, rubbing her head.

Afterwards, Leah said, "He sounded a little bit hopeful, don't you think?"

"Not hopeful enough," said Quincy grimly. "I'm going to have to organize something myself. Or Rumpel Rebounders will go under, just like Rumpel Mushrooms did!"

# 8

# The Game

Saturday morning was drizzly and Mrs. Rumpel had to work, being by now fully recovered from her accident. But she had strict instructions for her family, who were all going to watch Morris's soccer game.

"Warm him up in the car whenever you can," she said. "And be sure to give him this hot soup out of the Thermos."

"Nobody has soup at a soccer game," protested Morris. "We just eat our oranges."

"You'll eat soup today. And Quincy, I'd like you to take your poncho. If you see Morris standing around in the rain, put him in it."

"MAAA!" bleated Morris.

"Have a heart!" cried Quincy.

"It might keep him from getting pneumonia. Quincy, I'm depending on you to look after him."

"I don't even know where that dumb poncho is," muttered Quincy after her mother had left.

"I do," said Leah. "You put it behind the wood pile in the basement."

Just as they were ready to leave, the phone rang. "I'll get it," cried Quincy, putting down Morris's Thermos of soup and grabbing the phone. "It might be Desmond. Maybe the game's been cancelled or something."

"Halloooo," she said in a husky drawl. "This is the Rumpel residence. Quincy Rumpel speaking. Whom may I say is calling?"

There was silence at the other end for a moment. Then Gwen asked, "Quincy? Is that you?"

"Of course it's me," growled Quincy. "I just said it was."

After they had arranged to pick up Gwen, there was a second call. This time Mr. Rumpel answered it. It seemed he had forgotten to deliver some Rumpel Rebounders to a shopping centre. "I'll have to take them over," he told the family. "I'll drive you all to the game, and I'll pick you up after."

"Don't forget Chucky," Morris told his father as they got in the station wagon. "And Gwen," said Quincy.

"Hey, look! We've got snakes on our windshield!" squealed Morris from the front seat.

"What?" screamed Leah.

"Snakes. You know, windshield vipers!" And Morris collapsed in a fit of giggles. His shoulders were still shaking when they stopped at the corner to pick up Chucky.

"You boys will have quite a cheering section today," remarked Mr. Rumpel as they stopped for Gwen. Wearing her white fur-trimmed parka and clutching three umbrellas and some new garbage bags, she was waiting on her front verandah.

"These umbrellas are brand new," she said, struggling into the back seat between Leah and Quincy. "But they're seconds, so they might just have a tiny hole somewhere, Daddy says. I also brought garbage bags to sit on because I'm wearing my good pants."

"Good idea," admitted Quincy, who hadn't even thought of wet benches. The only rain gear she'd brought was the rubber poncho, and it was huddled in the bottom of a plastic shopping bag. She had no intention of using it.

They pulled up beside the soccer field and everyone spilled out of the car. Clad in their yellow jerseys and short pants, Morris and Chucky scooted off to join their teammates, while the girls looked for the best place to sit. "As close to Morris's team as we can get," directed Quincy.

Spreading out the green garbage bags, the girls sat down on a bench and opened Gwen's umbrellas.

"Is he here? Do you see him?" asked Quincy, trying to see through her rain-splattered glasses.

"I see him!" cried Leah. "He's talking to Morris."

"I wonder if he sees us," said Quincy.

Gwen shook her head. "His glasses are too muddy."

The rain let up just before the game started, much to everyone's relief. Gwen's umbrellas did have holes, after all.

They cheered loudly for Morris's team and Quincy added her specialty—a shrill two-fingered whistle. But it became apparent before long that Morris wasn't playing with his usual gusto.

"He looks worried," observed Quincy. Morris, in fact, looked anguished. He kept twitching his behind and tugging at his shorts.

"He's only kicked the ball once—and that wasn't very good," said Leah. "Even Mom could have done better."

Eventually Morris was replaced by another player and dispatched to the bench. As he sat there morosely, Quincy said, "He's even sitting funny."

The three girls walked over to him. "What's the matter with you?" asked Quincy.

"I don't know," replied Morris, "My shorts hurt, and I can't bend."

"Maybe he's got a hernia," suggested Gwen.

"Have you?" Quincy asked him. "Have you got one of those?"

"I don't even know what they are," said Morris. Neither did Gwen, it turned out.

"Is he all right?" asked a new voice. Quincy turned around to see who was speaking. There was Desmond. He was talking to her!

As she gazed into his muddy glasses, Quincy got tongue-tied. For once in her life she couldn't speak.

It was Gwen who finally answered. "Morris can't bend," she said, fluffing her hair. "And his shorts hurt."

Standing Morris up, the coach looked him over. "I think I see your trouble," he said. "Try turning your shorts around. They're on backwards."

"Not in front of everybody!" squealed Morris. "I can't do that in front of everybody!"

"The poncho!" spluttered Quincy.

"Yeah," said Leah. "Put him under the poncho to change and no one will see him!"

"What poncho?" asked Gwen as Quincy splashed back to their bench to retrieve it. When she returned, Desmond had gone.

"Can you believe it?" cried Quincy, shaking out her green rubber birthday present. "He was actually talking to me, and all I said was 'The poncho!' "

"Actually," said Gwen, helping to hold the slippery garment over Morris, "he was quite easy to talk to."

"Huh!"

"Keep holding it over my head so nobody can see me!" Morris's voice sounded muffled as he squirmed and grunted in his makeshift tent. At last he emerged. "That sure feels better," he said, bounding joyfully off to rejoin the game.

At half-time the drizzle started again. Morris appeared, covered in mud. "Where's my soup?" he demanded.

"You'd better give him his soup," said Leah.

Quincy groped under the bench. "I set it down when I answered the phone this morning. I must have left it there," she said at last. "It sure isn't here."

"You forgot my soup?" Morris wailed.

"What's the big deal?" said Quincy. "You said you wouldn't eat it anyway."

"Well, I feel like having some now."

"Well, you can't. I forgot it, period. Eat your orange."

"I'm telling! You forgot on purpose. And you're supposed to warm me up in the car, Mom said."

"How can I, you little jerk? The car's not here. Just get back to your game, unless you want to be warmed up in the poncho." Morris skittered off.

During the second half the rain started again. As the girls sat huddled under their umbrellas,

Gwen whispered, "I think Desmond is coming over here!"

"I see him, I see him!" hissed Quincy. She cleared her throat and brushed a wad of wet hair out of her eyes.

"I know this is kind of nervy ..." began Desmond, looking at Quincy.

"Oh, no!" she interrupted. "Au contraire! It's not nervy at all!" She stood up quickly, knocking Desmond's glasses off with her umbrella.

Picking them up off the wet grass, Desmond set them back on his nose. "I was just wondering, if you weren't using that poncho, if I could borrow it until after the game?"

"The poncho?" cried Quincy. "You want to borrow the poncho?"

"Only if you kids aren't using it. I get so danged wet standing out there. And I have a date right after the game. I just don't want to look like a drowned rat!"

"Oh, sure." Quincy choked out the words. Reaching under the bench she hauled out the poncho and gave it to him.

"Thanks, kids," he said, shrugging himself into the voluminous folds. "This is a great rig. Is it your dad's?"

"No," mumbled Quincy. "It's mine."

As Desmond strode back to the game with the poncho flopping about his ankles, Gwen remarked, "It's too long for him, isn't it?"

"Yeah," agreed Quincy. "He's actually pretty short. Personally, I prefer tall men."

Due in part to Morris kicking the ball between the wrong goalposts, his team lost.

"But I kicked it almost six yards," said Morris, as he joined the three girls after the game. "That was pretty good, wasn't it?"

"Sure it was," said Quincy.

When Mr. Rumpel arrived to pick up his family, he found them standing by the curb huddled under Gwen's leaky umbrellas.

"Well, how's our star soccer player?" he asked, as his soggy passengers packed themselves into the car.

"Okay," answered Morris. "We almost won."

Just as Mr. Rumpel was about to pull away from the curb, someone came running up and rapped on the back window.

Quincy opened it, and there stood Desmond. "Here," he said, thrusting an armful of wet green rubber at her. "I almost forgot to return your poncho. Thanks again!" Then he disappeared into the rain.

"What was that all about?" wondered Mr. Rumpel.

"Just somebody returning my poncho," said Quincy, heaving it into the back of the station wagon.

"So it did come in handy, after all."

"Kind of," said Quincy. "Let's go home now."

# 9

# The Last Halloween

"Guess what!" cried Quincy, bursting into the kitchen a few days later. "There's going to be a costume parade on Halloween, and the winners will be on TV!"

"But that's tomorrow," said Mrs. Rumpel. "Have you got a costume ready?"

"Sort of. It's in my mind. I'll just need to borrow a few things. Oh, boy! I've got to win this!"

"What about taking Morris trick-or-treating? You promised."

"We'll do that first. Gwen and I decided this will probably be our last year for going out on Halloween, so we'll all go. Then we'll go to the school for the costume parade."

As Quincy stood contemplating the contents of the refrigerator, the front door slammed and Leah and Morris came in.

"Ma," cried Morris, "I have to be a skeleton for tomorrow night!"

"Don't tempt me," muttered Quincy.

"A skeleton?" Mrs. Rumpel looked surprised. "But I thought you were going to be a hockey player. How can I make a skeleton suit by tomorrow night?"

"I was going to be Gretzky, but now I changed my mind. Chucky's gonna be Dracula, with bloody fangs and everything, so I want to be a real scary skeleton." Discovering a bowl of leftover spaghetti in the refrigerator, Morris scuttled over to the table with it and soon had it devoured.

"I hope you haven't changed *your* mind, Leah," said her mother. "Aunt Ida gave me some nice lace curtains to make you a ballet outfit."

"Gee, thanks, Mom. But I was thinking if it wasn't too much trouble, I'd sooner be a witch. Quincy loaned me her false nose, but I still need a long black skirt. Have you got one?"

"Mom, I need a stem for my head," added Quincy.

"A stem?"

"Yeah, you know! Like, a squash stem or something?"

"Maybe if you told us what you were planning to be, I could help more," said her mother.

"But I can't take a chance of the wrong people finding out my costume," said Quincy. "If I win, I'll be famous. Then Rumpel Rebounders will be famous, and Dad will sell lots of them."

"Well," sighed Mrs. Rumpel, "maybe you could stuff a sock with crumpled paper for a stem. That might work."

"Good idea!" said Quincy. "Oh, you know that old orange tablecloth that got mildewed in the ironing pile? Can I have it?"

"I suppose so."

"Oh, boy, I can't wait. I just know I'm gonna win!"

"I hope you do, dear."

"Mom?" It was Leah. "About that black skirt?"

"Yes, I have one," said her mother. "Come upstairs with me, and we'll find it."

"Skeleton suit! Skeleton suit!" Morris reminded her.

"I haven't forgotten," said Mrs. Rumpel.

Emerging only long enough to eat dinner, Quincy closeted herself in her room to make her costume. Not even Leah was permitted in.

"It's not fair, you know," said Leah. "That room's half mine."

"I'm almost done."

Finally, at ten o'clock, Mrs. Rumpel insisted that Leah be let in to go to bed. "Bed for you, too, Quincy!" she said. "You'll have to finish it tomorrow."

A loud groan emerged from the bedroom, followed by much scurrying about. At last Quincy opened the door. There were snips of orange cloth all over the floor and the pillows were missing from the two beds.

"Where's my pillow?" demanded Leah.

"I meant to ask you if I could borrow it," said Quincy. "Just till after Halloween. Please? The whole future of Rumpel Rebounders may depend on your pillow!"

"I don't even know what you're doing with it!" wailed Leah.

"Just trust me!"

Putting her long black skirt, an old witch's hat and Quincy's false nose carefully beside her bed, Leah settled herself as comfortably as she could and soon was fast asleep.

After tossing and turning for a while, Quincy finally got up and turned on the light again. Retrieving a bundle of orange material from the back of the cupboard, she sat up in bed and continued sewing her costume. She was, after all, technically in bed, she reasoned.

The next night it was already dark when Gwen arrived at six o'clock. To save her feet, she had been driven over by Uncle George. She was wearing a trim white ski suit, white crash helmet with NASA across the front, and a pair of Aunt Ida's high-heeled white boots.

"Wow!" exclaimed Leah when she opened the door. "Who are you supposed to be?"

"Sally Ride, the female astronaut," replied Gwen. "Where did you get that nose? I've never seen one like that before."

"It's Quincy's. Isn't it great? She got it when we lived in Toronto. Don't they have this kind out here?"

"Not exactly. Where's Quincy?"

"Upstairs, but you can't go up. She won't let anyone see her yet. Mom's in the kitchen painting Morris's bones. You can go and see them." As she started to follow Gwen, Leah tripped on the hem of her long black skirt, and had to stop to roll it up at the waist. This produced a thick wad about her middle, and revealed un-witchlike grubby joggers and striped socks.

Gwen tottered on her high-heeled boots out to the kitchen where a Dracula perched on the table and a skeleton was being prepared.

"Hi, everybody!" said Gwen.

"Hi," said Morris and Chucky. Mrs. Rumpel, immersed in her task, merely grunted. Morris, wearing a pair of Leah's old black tights and a black sweatshirt, was standing on a chair while his mother painted white bones on him with poster paint.

"Don't forget my funny bones, Ma," giggled Morris.

"Those are very good tibias and fibulas, Aunt Rose," said Gwen.

Mrs. Rumpel glanced up at Gwen. "Elvis!" she exclaimed. "Elvis Presley!"

"Sally Ride," corrected Gwen. "I'm Sally Ride, the female astronaut!"

"Hurry up, Ma, or we'll miss all the good candy," bleated Morris.

"Sometimes when people run out of candy, they give you money," commented Chucky.

"They do?" cried Morris. "Did you hear that, Mom? Boy, I'm sure glad we moved out here!"

Mrs. Rumpel smudged around Morris's eyes with black, giving him dark eye sockets, and covered his face and lips with white make-up.

"Oh, boy, I look great!" cried Morris happily, after adding a white bathing cap to his ensemble.

Going to the foot of the stairs, Mrs. Rumpel called, "Hurry up, Quincy! Everybody's ready!"

There was a squeak at the top of the stairs.

"Here she comes!" cried Morris.

Clutching her ballooning stomach so her pillows wouldn't slip, Quincy descended the stairs. She was wearing what appeared to be giant orange knickers. Stuffed with pillows, they sagged almost to her knees, dangerously straining the red suspenders that supported them.

Her legs were encased in green tights and she wore her orange turtleneck sweater. A stuffed brown sock was pinned to a green baseball cap on her head, and for a finishing touch, Quincy had painted two eyes on her cheeks.

"Ta-*daaa*!" she cried.

"WOW!" gasped Morris.

"What are you?" asked Chucky.

"I'm a pumpkin, dummy," replied Quincy. Then she noticed Gwen, slim and trim in her white outfit.

"I'm Sally Ride," said Gwen. "The female astronaut."

"I know who she is!" said Quincy crossly, flouncing to the door with her orange knickers billowing and her brown stem wobbling.

Once outside, Chucky and Morris scuttled ahead while the three girls tripped, tottered and billowed down the street after them. When they had finished trick-or-treating on that block of Tulip Street, Quincy said, "Okay. Now it's costume parade time. Everybody to the school!"

"Thank goodness!" cried Gwen. "These boots are killing me!"

At the school they found hundreds of small and strange creatures milling around in the gym, shepherded for the most part by their parents.

"Good grief," said Quincy. "It's wall to wall with infants!"

"You're not going in the costume parade with all those little kids, are you?" Gwen asked.

"I sure am. Look at those TV cameras over there! I'm not going to miss this opportunity. I think I have a good chance of winning. I'm the only pumpkin here."

"Well, I'm not going in it." Gwen hobbled over to a bench and sat down.

"Here I go!" cried Quincy, hitching up her bloomers. She strode toward the line-up accompanied by Leah, whose hat elastic had broken.

As the vampires, ghosts and skeletons, witches, monsters and storybook characters shuffled past the judges, one lone orange pumpkin bobbed along majestically, towering over the others.

Then they lined up in front of the gym.

At last the judges were ready to announce their decision. Waving gaily to Gwen, Quincy hitched up her knickers and prepared to step forward.

A few minutes later she was standing on the sidelines with Gwen, watching the cameras zoom in on the three winners. "I can't believe this is happening!" said Quincy. There on the stage in front of everyone, flushed with victory, were a Little Bo-Peep, an aluminum covered robot and, grinning broadly behind his plastic fangs, Chucky.

# 10

# The Birthday

That night, long after Leah had fallen asleep, Quincy lay awake thinking. Eventually she got up and opened the curtains, then hopped back into bed again.

In the moonlight she could see the last leaves on the cherry tree twisting and spinning in the wind. They would soon fall, Quincy thought. She felt like a leaf just about ready to let go. Tomorrow she would be twelve.

All at once, and for the first time in her life, Quincy wasn't in a hurry for her birthday to come. Things were bound to be different. She probably wouldn't go trick-or-treating ever again, or be in the costume parade.

She thought about her father and Rumpel Rebounders. It seemed as if he wasn't getting any closer to advertising them on television. Maybe if she got a unicycle for her birthday tomorrow, she would practise and get to be so good that the News Hour would come and interview her. "This is

Quincy, they would say, the most athletic of the Rumpel athletes, who owe all their success to training on the fabulous Rumpel Rebounders … ''

Eventually Quincy fell asleep. Toward morning she began to dream. She dreamt Snowflake was holding a hula hoop and she was jumping through it, dressed in a golden crash helmet, high-heeled white boots and her orange bloomers.

Suddenly she woke up. Somebody was punching her on the shoulder and shouting, ''Happy birthday!''

''Huh? Whazzit?'' mumbled Quincy, sitting up.

''You were really dreaming,'' said Leah. ''You were twitching and talking like anything!''

''What did I say?''

''A lot of junk I couldn't understand, and then you said, 'One giant jump for mankind!' and you started sort of barking.''

''Oh, yeah. I remember now. I was jumping through a hula hoop.''

''Anyways, here's your present,'' said Leah, handing her a small package wrapped in slightly used Christmas wrapping paper.

''Oh, boy, thanks!'' cried Quincy, ripping it open.

''It's a real dog brush,'' said Leah.

''It's just what we need!'' As Snowflake was asleep in Morris's room, Quincy tried the brush out on her own hair. "I wouldn't mind one of these myself," she said.

She hurried downstairs and rapidly inspected the house. There was no unicycle. But she did get a book of dog stories, a new pair of joggers and a yellow jumpsuit from her parents. There was a flower-covered purple sweatshirt and a book, *How to Train Your Dog*, from Aunt Fan, and a money belt from Morris. "It's not real leather," he said. "It only looks like it."

As her children left for school that morning, Mrs. Rumpel kissed them goodbye. "I hope you haven't got band practice or anything tonight," she said to Quincy. "Aunt Ida and Uncle George and Gwen are coming over for your birthday supper."

"There's no band tonight," replied Quincy, who was dressed in all her new birthday finery. "But I might be a bit late if I get thrown in the showers."

"Thrown in the showers?" cried Mrs. Rumpel.

"Yeah. I might be," she said hopefully. "When you're a senior they sometimes do that on your birthday. If they like you."

That night, when the Other Rumpels arrived for the family dinner, they brought more presents for Quincy. Aunt Ida and Uncle George brought her a box of chocolates and a red umbrella in its own little tote bag. Gwen gave her a poster with five white puppies on it, and an inflatable bath pillow.

Mrs. Rumpel had cooked Quincy's favourite meal, chicken and dumplings. Then, while everybody sang "Happy Birthday," she carried in a birthday cake ablaze with twelve candles. It was covered with chocolate icing, decorated here and there with little blobs of white.

"Mom, it's beautiful. I love the little roses!" exclaimed Quincy.

"They're dogs," said her mother. "Samoyeds." And she set the cake down in front of Quincy.

"Make a wish!" everybody cried.

Quincy took a deep breath. She didn't have to think about a wish. She'd had it ready all day. Letting go with one big puff, she not only blew out the candles, she blew them over.

"Well, at least I'll get my wish," she said, picking the candles off one by one and licking them.

All in all, it had been a good birthday, she thought, gazing happily around the table. She had even got dunked in the showers at school. Tonight she would have a leisurely bath, reclining on her inflatable bath pillow and reading one of her new books while she ate chocolates. Tomorrow morning she would give Snowflake a good brushing, and wear her new clothes to school again.

Maybe growing older wasn't going to be so bad after all.

# 11

# The Plan

The next day Quincy was late getting home from school. When Leah and Morris arrived without her, Mrs. Rumpel asked, "What's keeping your sister today?"

"They were having tryouts for the school play. Gwen and her both stayed," said Leah.

"Gwen and she," said Mrs. Rumpel absently. She was leaning out the kitchen window pouring birdseed into the feeder, while in the bushes below an army of sparrows waited silently.

"Well, anyways, they both stayed to try out for parts."

"Didn't you want to be in it?"

"It's mostly the drama club, and they're mostly the big kids. We get to watch the rehearsals sometimes, though," said Leah.

"We don't," said Morris, making himself a pickle sandwich. "Us little kids don't get any breaks."

"*We*," sighed his mother. "*We* little kids!" As she closed the window, the sparrows converged on the feeder in full battle cry, to the accompaniment of the wind chimes. The hullaballoo was so great as the birds jostled and shoved for position, that Mrs. Rumpel finally closed the curtains. "At least we don't have to look at them!" she said.

The Rumpels were just starting supper when they heard the front door slam, and Quincy came in.

"Did you get a part?" asked Leah.

Quincy's cheeks were pink, and her glasses were steamed up because she had run home. "Oh, boy! Did I get a part!" she cried, throwing off her jacket and washing her hands.

"Your dinner's in the oven," said her mother. "You sound as if you got an important part. Are you the leading lady, maybe?"

"Maybe she's the leading man, ha-ha-ha!" chortled Morris.

"There isn't any real leading lady," Quincy told them. "But I'm sort of the star!"

"That's great!" said Mr. Rumpel.

"I have to study my part right after supper," said Quincy. "Is it all right if I use the living room?"

"Can we watch?" asked Leah.

"No, I have to do it in private."

"Well, if you need to, dear," said Mrs. Rumpel. "Go ahead. Leah and Morris will do the dishes tonight."

"That's not fair," grumbled Morris.

"Your sister has an important part to study for," said Mrs. Rumpel. "She's a star!"

Quincy gulped down her supper and then disappeared into the front room. She closed the sliding double doors to the dining room behind her.

"I never knew she was interested in acting," remarked Mr. Rumpel.

"She probably gets it from the Twistle side of the family," said Mrs. Rumpel. "I used to recite a lot in school—I was quite good, too. 'By the shores of Gitche Gumee, By the shining Big-Sea-Water ... ' "

"Mom!" wailed Leah.

"Quincy's not saying anything like that," reported Morris from the dining room, where he was peering through the crack between the sliding doors.

Putting her ear against them, Leah whispered, "I don't hear anything at all."

"She's probably still studying the part," said Mrs. Rumpel. "I remember how I used to have to prepare for my recitations when ... "

"I wanna go in there and watch TV," Morris whined.

"Why can't she rehearse in her bedroom?" wondered Mr. Rumpel. "I would like to watch the news."

"Sssh, don't disturb her," said Mrs. Rumpel. "Wait, I think I hear something!" The four Rumpels clustered around the door, listening.

Slowly, a low, gurgling sound began to be heard. "Aaaaarrrrgggghhh ... "

Then suddenly it became a strangled bellow. "AAAARRRRGGGGGGGHHHHH!"

Grabbing one of his doorknobs from the plate rail, Mr. Rumpel flung open the sliding doors and stormed the living room, closely followed by the rest of the family.

Quincy was lying sprawled across the rebounder. "What's the matter?" she asked.

"What's the matter?" repeated her father. "What's the matter? Maybe you'd better tell us!"

"I was practising my part, that's all."

"*That* was your part?" Mrs. Rumpel looked dumbfounded.

"Sure. That was me falling into the abyss. We're doing 'Theseus and the Minotaur' and I'm the minotaur. In ancient Greece. Freddie Twikenham— he's Theseus—slays me and rescues all the maidens and youths. Gwen is a maiden. It's an old sort of legend. I love it!"

"Couldn't you have been a maiden?" wondered Mrs. Rumpel.

"But I'm the star! They needed somebody tall to be the minotaur, and I'm it!"

"What's a minotaur?" asked Morris. "Something like a brontosaurus?"

"Not that big, dummy. Just a sort of average-sized monster. All I do is stomp around and make noises. Then at the end, when Freddie slays me, I fall into the abyss. It's the best part I've ever had in my entire life. Wait till you see my costume!"

"Maybe you could wear it for Halloween next year," suggested Leah.

"I'm through with Halloween," replied Quincy. "From now on I'm doing bigger things."

"Oh, boy," said Morris. "Wait till I tell Chucky that you're going to be a greasy monster."

"But I still don't understand why you have to practise in the living room," said Mr. Rumpel, settling down in his easy chair to watch the news.

Quincy sighed. "It's because of the rebounder," she explained patiently. "You see, when I fall into my abyss I have to land on something, so I may as well land on something bouncy, like the rebounder."

Later that night, Quincy lay on her bed with her hands clasped behind her head, thinking. Suddenly she cried, "I've got it!"

"Got what?" asked Leah, looking up from brushing Snowflake, who was lying on his back with his feet in the air.

"A plan. How to help Dad advertise the re-bounders! It's perfect! You know how we're having printed programs and everything for the play. Well, I'll just take one of our rebounders to the school and put it in my abyss. Then they can print it in the program. MINI-TRAMPOLINE USED IN THE ABYSS SUPPLIED BY RUMPEL RE-BOUNDERS. Dad will get all that free advertising, and everybody will want to buy one!"

"I knew you'd think of something," said Leah. "Are you sure they'll let you do it?"

"I'll bet Miss Dingwall will, and she's in charge of the drama club. Besides, it's my abyss. I'm the one who has to fall into it! But don't tell Mom and Dad. I want to surprise them."

"Maybe we'll be rich after all," said Leah, hugging Snowflake.

The next day Quincy found Leah in the lunch room at noon. "It's all set," she said. "Miss Dingwall thinks it's a good idea, and she's going to put it in the program. Oh, boy, Rumpel Rebounders will sell like hotcakes after this!"

The play was to be presented in the evening, on the last day of school before the Christmas holidays.

That day, Quincy came home early in the afternoon to get ready. As she burst in the door she cried, "Guess what, Mom! Guess what's going to happen at the play tonight!"

Mrs. Rumpel couldn't.

"We're going to be on TV! The News Hour is going to be there filming us. I knew my birthday wish would come true when I blew out all those candles!"

"Be sure and wash your hair," said Mrs. Rumpel. "They might interview you afterwards, being the star and all."

"You betcha!" said Quincy, disappearing upstairs.

# 12

# And Finally, the Action

All the family except Quincy were sitting at the table waiting for their supper. "This will be the first time a Rumpel has been the star in a play!" remarked Mrs. Rumpel as she dished up the mashed potatoes.

"And this is one time we won't be late!" said her husband. "Hurry up with your meal, everybody, and don't dawdle."

"How can we dawdle when we haven't got our food yet?" Morris wanted to know.

"I'm coming, I'm coming!" said Mrs. Rumpel, scooping the mashed potatoes back into the pot.

"Mother!" cried Leah.

"You'd better help her," advised Mr. Rumpel. "Your mother's not herself tonight."

"Isn't Quincy down yet?" asked Mrs. Rumpel as she put the plates on the table.

"She's upstairs, doing her eyelashes," answered Leah.

"She's been doing them since four o'clock," said Morris.

"Quincy, come down here and have your supper!" hollered Mrs. Rumpel.

"I'm not hungry!"

"I'll eat hers," offered Morris.

"No, you won't," said his mother. "Quincy, you have to eat something!"

In a few minutes Quincy appeared. Her hair was freshly shampooed and her eyelashes delicately darkened with her mother's mascara. She had cleaned her glasses, and she wore her new yellow jumpsuit.

"You look splendid!" said Mr. Rumpel, who was drinking his coffee standing up, to save time.

Mrs. Rumpel nodded approvingly. "You look lovely, dear. Now please eat something."

"Honest, Mom, I can't. My stomach's in knots."

Mrs. Rumpel sighed. "Well, at least have a drink of milk."

As she poured herself a glass of milk, Quincy grumbled, "When I have kids I'm never going to make them eat when they don't want to."

At last everybody was ready. Hurrying out of the house, they piled into the station wagon. As they headed toward the school, something hurtled over the back seat and landed on Quincy's lap.

"Snowflake! Did you sneak into the car again?" cried Morris.

"He's just so happy to see us!" said Leah, giving him a hug.

"He'd love to watch the play, I bet," said Quincy hopefully.

"We're not taking that dog into the school," her father said. "No way."

As they pulled into the parking lot, Mrs. Rumpel cried, "I knew we'd be too early! We didn't have to rush like that. We're the first ones here."

There was no one in the gym except for two boys setting out chairs. The Rumpels sat down in the front row. Quincy went to get ready.

It wasn't long before they were joined by Aunt Ida and Uncle George. "Gwen's gone backstage to get dressed," said Aunt Ida. "She has the darlingest costume! I spent hours making it. And she looks so good in white. I just hope that she won't catch cold in her bare feet."

"I hear they're going to televise the performance," said Uncle George.

As the seats around them filled up, Mrs. Rumpel said in a loud voice, "Did you know our Quincy's the star?"

Suddenly Morris began waving to someone behind them. "It's the Murphys!" he cried. "They said they were coming to see Quincy, and here they are! They're almost right behind us.''

As the Rumpels turned around to wave to their neighbours, Mrs. Rumpel suddenly fluttered a program under her husband's nose. ''Look at this! It says, 'Starring Quincy Rumpel as the Minotaur' right on the very front!'' And she began to sniffle happily.

''But did you see this?'' cried Mr. Rumpel, pointing to the bottom of the page. ''Mini-trampoline courtesy of Rumpel Rebounders! Quincy must have done it,'' he said thoughtfully. ''What do you know about that!''

''That's a nice bit of publicity,'' said Uncle George approvingly.

''Here come the TV people!'' announced Morris, standing up to see them better.

''Ssssh, sit down,'' said his mother.

Miss Dingwall, in a red dress with a pattern of little green turkeys, made her way across the stage in front of the long velvet curtains. Everyone was quiet as she welcomed the audience and told them about the play.

''It's going to be good,'' whispered Morris loudly. ''It's all about creeps.''

''Crete,'' corrected his mother.

''Sssssh!'' hissed Aunt Ida.

The gym lights went out and the curtains parted. Out onto the stage danced twelve barefoot maidens. They wore white net dresses and had plastic flowers in their hair. Then six youths shuffled out in their gym shorts.

"Heh, heh," chortled Mr. Rumpel. "The youths seem a little overpowered by all those hefty maidens!"

"Sssssh!" whispered his wife.

"There's Gwen," said Aunt Ida proudly.

"That's Freddie Twikenham." Leah pointed to the shortest and plumpest of the youths. "He's Theseus."

"How come there's not enough boys?" Morris wanted to know.

"None of them wanted to do it if they couldn't be Theseus and slay the monster," answered Leah in a hoarse whisper. "Miss Dingwall could only get six boys."

Across the back of the stage, tables had been draped in brown canvas to represent winding subterranean passages.

"It's the labyrinth," whispered Mrs. Rumpel.

"What's a labyrinth?" asked Morris.

"Sssssssh!" said Aunt Ida.

Suddenly from somewhere offstage came a gargly growl. "I hear Quincy!" said Morris.

"Watch," whispered Leah. "Quincy's going to come out now!"

As the dancing youths and maidens suddenly huddled in a cluster at one side of the stage, everyone fell silent. Then, as the audience gasped, heavy clumpings were heard approaching. The minotaur appeared.

"*Wow*!" gasped Morris. "A cow!"

Quincy's upper half was disguised with a huge brown mask of a bull, complete with horns and a gaping red mouth. Her bottom half, clad in brown pantyhose, was only slightly more recognizable.

"Good grief!" exclaimed Mrs. Rumpel.

"Where's the rest of her costume?" asked Morris.

"A minotaur," explained Mr. Rumpel, "was supposed to be half bull and half man."

"Sssh!" whispered Aunt Ida.

The play progressed to the last act. There the monster, prowling along on one of the tables, was finally dealt the fatal blow by Freddy.

"AAAARRRRRGGGGHHH!" roared Quincy, as she plunged off the table into her abyss. The audience cheered and whistled. The television cameras whirred.

Theseus raised his arms over his head in victory. Then the youths and maidens broke out of their huddle and began to skip about the stage.

Suddenly the minotaur reappeared.

Bouncing back up out of the abyss into full view, it waved cheerfully to the audience and did a quick scissor-kick with its brown legs before vanishing again.

The cameramen, anticipating another appearance, kept their cameras aimed at the abyss. Sure enough, the minotaur soared into view once more—not quite so high this time—and then was seen no more.

The maidens and youths proceeded with their victory dance. But after the finale of the minotaur, it was somewhat of an anticlimax.

As the blue velvet curtains slowly jerked together, Miss Dingwall herded the cast out in front. Everyone clapped as the six youths and twelve maidens joined hands and took their bows. Behind them stood the minotaur. Suddenly, doing a little jig—something like a sword dance—it began to wave and blow kisses. The audience cheered wildly.

When the applause subsided, the cast leaped down from the stage to find their families. Peering shortsightedly through the eye-holes of the mask, Quincy charged through the crowd. Suddenly she found herself staring into a TV camera.

"Tell us how you managed that double-bounce, Minotaur!" asked a reporter.

"Moi?" The minotaur jabbed itself in the chest with a front hoof.

"Yes, you. You stole the show, you know."

"Ackshully," Quincy's voice was a little muffled due to the papier-mâché mask, "ackshully, it wash eashy. I wash ushing a Rumpelsh Rebounder."

"Did you hear that, folks?" said the reporter. "Our minotaur was using a Rumpel Rebounder. Well, it certainly had a lot of bounce!" Then, turning to the cameraman, he said, "That's a wrap, Clyde."

"When will it be on TV?" several people wanted to know.

"Just be sure and watch the late evening news tonight," the reporter told them. "You'll see your friendly minotaur in action again!" Then he and the cameraman disappeared into the crowd.

"Oh, boy!" cried the minotaur. "I'm gonna be on the newsh, Mom!"

"I'm so proud of you, dear," said Mrs. Rumpel, squeezing Quincy's paw, while Mr. Rumpel patted her lumpy brown shoulders.

"It shure ish hot in thish thing!" Struggling out of the cumbersome mask, Quincy emerged red-faced and sticky-haired just in time to greet the Murphys.

"We just wanted to congratulate you," they said as they rushed up. "We're going to hurry home to watch you on the news. This is very exciting!" And they rushed away.

Suddenly everybody was in a hurry to leave, so as not to miss the news. As the Rumpels made their way out of the gym, Mrs. Rumpel darted around picking up discarded programs to send to their relatives. "Won't they be surprised!" she said.

When they got to their car, they found Snowflake sitting in the driver's seat, looking bored. "Oh, poor Snowflake!" cried Quincy. "We forgot all about you!"

Mr. Rumpel unlocked the car, but before anyone else got in, he took Quincy's arm and ushered her grandly into the front seat.

"After all," he said, "we've never had a star in the family before!"

"Do you think the rebounders will sell better now?" asked Quincy.

"Like hotcakes, Princess, like hotcakes!" said Mr. Rumpel.

Mrs. Rumpel rode home in the back seat between Leah and Morris, and with most of Snowflake on her lap. "Did anyone remember to feed this dog before we left home?" she asked.

"Oh, no!" groaned the Rumpel chorus. "We forgot!"

"Poor Snowflake. He must be starving!" cried Leah.

"*I* sure am," declared Morris.

"Moi, too!" said Quincy Rumpel, the star.

## The End

# *Collect the Quincy Rumpel series!*

## Quincy Rumpel

Quincy Rumpel wants pierced ears, curly hair and a Save-the-Whales T-shirt.

Her sister, Leah, can't see why she shouldn't have pierced ears, too, while Morris, her brother, longs for a dog.

Mrs. Rumpel hopes for rain, so her job at the umbrella shop will thrive.

And the neighbours, the Murphys, just can't decide whether having the Rumpels next door is the best or the worst thing that ever happened to them.

ISBN 0-88899-036-7 $5.95 paperback

## Quincy Rumpel, P.I.

Why is Quincy Rumpel creeping around the old Bean-blossom house? Has she discovered the bizarre burial ground of the little dog, Nanki-poo? And what are the strange apparitions that her brother, Morris, sees in the house at night? How about the treasure that Captain Beanblossom left behind? And, most important, who else is interested in the abandoned house?

Quincy Rumpel is back again with an all-woman private investigating firm. But her best-laid plans soon go astray when she's joined by ever-bothersome Morris, his best friend, Chucky, and her heart-throb, Freddie Twikenham, who is convinced that he has his grandfather's Mountie blood coursing through his veins.

ISBN 0-88899-081-2 $5.95 paperback

# Morris Rumpel and the Wings of Icarus

Morris Rumpel, youngest member of the crazy and unpredictable Rumpel family, is on his way to the sleepy little town of Cranberry Corners to visit his grandparents for the summer. The trip brings surprises and adventures, from Morris's first airplane flight as an Unaccompanied Minor, to his attempt to learn to ride Fireweed (a horse with a mind of her own!), and a friendship with a family of peregrine falcons that live near his grandparent's farm.

But the vacation turns out to hold more adventure than even Morris has bargained for. It begins the moment he is followed off the plane by a mysterious, icicle-eyed stranger, and the plot thickens as Morris gradually realizes that his new friends, the falcons, are in deadly danger . . .

ISBN 0-88899-099-5 $5.95 paperback

# Quincy Rumpel and the Sasquatch of Phantom Cove

It all starts the day the Rumpels receive an invitation to visit their dear friends, Bert and Ernie, at their fishing resort on the west coast. As Quincy and her family happily pack up the old stationwagon with beach gear, fishing poles and their trusty dog, Snowflake, they imagine lazy summer days spent lying on the dock, fishing and eating fresh salmon in the resort dining room.

But more than one mystery awaits them. The resort is a rundown dump, the Rumpels are the only guests, and there are no fish! When Quincy, Leah and Morris set out to discover why the fish have so mysteriously disappeared they find signs of a very odd creature— a creature that looks a lot like a sasquatch!

ISBN 0-88899-129-0 $6.95 paperback

## Quincy Rumpel and the Woolly Chaps

Quincy Rumpel—Ranch Nanny

This job title sounds great to Quincy Rumpel, who has just moved to Cranberry Corners with her family to help run her grandparents' ranch. She's desperate to buy a horse, and what could be difficult about taking care of a bunch of kids?

She soon discovers that the McAddams family is even crazier than the Rumpels and even more prone to disaster!

ISBN 0-88899-160-6 $6.95 paperback